To Chindilani

*for her writerly
generosity*

TIDELANDS
PART 3

STAGE OF FOOLS

GARETH J. SOUTHWELL

ABOUT TIDELANDS

Tidelands is an ongoing sci-fi & fantasy serial currently being published every Friday on Substack. *Part 3: Stage of Fools* collects together episodes 35–50. Once you've finished, you can sign up here to follow the next episodes:

garethsouthwell.substack.com

TIDELANDS
PART 3

STAGE OF FOOLS

CHAPTER ONE

MOSTLY, SHE SLEEPS.

Fished from the waves – as they must have done, though Squirrel cannot now remember that – she wakes shackled, one hand, one foot, rattling the bed frame with the last dregs of panic. Gradually, her body blindly reports back the damage: a dull ache in her left forearm, another in her right thigh, a throbbing thickness to one half-closed eye and a stab to the ribs when she tries to sit up. A visual survey reveals the bandaging of lesser scratches and scrapes. She'll live. But what of her blue-eyed giant?

She is not always alone.

The medibots come and go, fussing, tending, changing her dressings, even asking if she needs anything – food, drink – their simulated voices modulated to a soporific whisper. "Let me go?" she suggests. To which they merely stare back impassively, their moulded plastic faces expressionless with incomprehension or non-compliance. That aside, they are polite, attentive jailers. In fact, once the restraints come off, it's all quite comfortable – even her own toilet, a shower – better than the Den, anyway; were it not for the periodically dissolving fourth wall, which is probably a one-way mirror too, opening up the room like a glass-fronted stage set for whoever wants to gawk at the freak.

But she has only one regular visitor.

Sometimes she wakes to find him leaning against the wall the other side of the glass, his silhouette merging with the shadows of the corridor. She cannot see behind his opaque black shades, and so all traffic is one-way: he can read her thoughts, but not she his – unless he wants her to.

[*You cannot win,*] he tells her one day – or night (there being no external window through which to tell one from the other). [*But I can help you, if you let me. I can train you.*]

They are not pleasant experiences, these little mental social calls; they are trespasses, violations, the breaking of another, far more intimate wall. It's how those she has invaded must have felt, consciously or not; like there is something crawling under your skin, burrowing away inside you like a parasite.

In response to his offer, she treats him to silent imaginings of his demise – the same in fact as she had tried to inflict on him: squished beneath Stegrun's enormous foot, or torn to shreds by nightmeerkats – but none of which have the least effect; on the contrary, he appears rather to enjoy it.

And only once, she sees the other man – the one who had done the deal with Denton in the eyrie, and whom she and the big blue giant had also tried to squish – and she immediately throws everything at him, spitting at the glass, mustering all the focus that her hatred and venom can fuel in an attempt to bore into his mind. But he doesn't even meet her eyes, merely laughs. He hasn't returned since.

How many days has it been? She's tried to count them, to set milestones in the desert of her captivity, but without the natural divisions of day and night to mark them apart, they blur together, dissolving into a seamless mass of time-stuff. They are drugging her, she's fairly sure. Early on, she pulls out the drip, flapping aside the gently worrying hands of the medibots, only to find it reinserted each time she reawakens, and she'll pull it out again. Eventually, sheer perseverance wins this little game, and in reward, unmasked, the brainfuzz gives way to the pain of her injuries. But at least that's real. At some point real food appears, probably drugged too. There then follows a different type of battle, where she is her own adversary. But there's only so long real hunger can be kept at bay, and after all, she decides, she does want to live. Which is something they seem to want too. So she eats the food and presumes the worst.

She is not the only prisoner; there are others, out of sight. Occasionally she hears them, a diversity of noises not quite categorisable – indistinct *somethings* that are not quite shouts and screeches, something akin to a moan or a growl, a whine, a scratch or a thump.

Her fellow inmates – if that's what they are – would appear to be nothing like her.

HE IS BACK AGAIN; this time, with a chair.

He places it before the glass, sits, and folds his hands neatly in front of him.

[*Look,*] he thinks.

But she moves her eyes away and down, back to the tablet from which she has been reading – a new placatory gift, along with a change of clothes, a hairbrush, toiletries, overnight gifts deposited unseen by her abductor Santa. The tablet doesn't have any network access, nothing she can hack, and anyway her implant is still offline, so no Feeds either. But it does contain books, films, games, and it's better than staring at the walls (dissolving, one-way-mirrored or otherwise). Maybe they're concerned that her brain won't rot, or at least that she doesn't smell.

[*Look,*] he repeats.

He removes his glasses.

His unadorned face is younger than expected, hairless and relatively unlined, giving him almost an innocent air. The eyes are of a pale grey, and if not kind, exactly, then not malign either; they are intelligent, seasoned – eyes that have seen things – and it is these that make him appear older than he probably is. She gears up to engage him, using the only weapon she has, to try to . . . What? For it's not a weapon she's ever used in malice, doesn't know how, and he just smirks.

[*We may not be friends,*] he tells her, [*but we need not be enemies.*]

Well, she'll see about that.

Their eyes connect, and – as best she can – she lunges at him with her mind.

And falls out of herself – is the best she can describe it.

Into a small square room, spartan and featureless, doors set into each wall. And at its centre sits the man.

[*I call this the airlock,*] his silent voice informs her, [*but you can name yours whatever you like. Think of it like an antechamber or a waiting room, where you can screen out uninvited guests.*]

She's never seen this before, never been in someone's mind as "they" stand there with you, aware of your presence. Mostly, her experiences have been PoVs, stolen first-person snapshots. But this is a constructed space, somewhere fashioned by a mind aware of its own dimensions.

[*Always imagine yourself as dressed comfortably,*] he continues. [*Your armour lies not in what you wear, but in your own alertness and composure. To maximise this, you must be as comfortable with your residual self-image as you can be. Be naked, if that's what makes you feel most at ease. This is what I used to wear when I was a kid.*] He gestures to his own attire. [*Back when I was happiest, I suppose, freest.*]

And, now she notices, gone is his customary black, replaced with a blue t-shirt with a faded logo, grey jogging bottoms, scuffed old trainers.

And where was that? she asks, surreptitiously trying one of the doors, which proves, unsurprisingly, locked – however that translates in psychic infosec. *When you were a kid?*

[*Nowhere you'd know. It's become a different country now, anyway; many different countries.*]

She tries another door, with the same result.

[*Would you like to see?*] he asks, and there is a chink of green-hued light as a door to his right springs ajar.

Is this some sort of trap? But she's already in one of those, isn't she? So why not?

She moves toward the open door and through they go together . . .

. . . INTO A LUSH green landscape, a rural idyll of rolling fields, their crests topped here and there with rows of teardrop trees that stripe shadows down the undulating slopes. Little red-roofed, white-walled buildings huddle together in small villages and towns, or else sit solitary upon their own hilltops that rise like islands out of the sea of morning mist. The sort of place people used to go on holiday, she's heard.

[*Well,*] he says, [*it used to be.*]

And in a blink they are in one of those little hilltop towns, treading its winding cobbled streets up to the square, with its cafes and market stalls and little sandstone church. Two boys are sitting on a kerb, playing some simple ancient game involving coloured stones. They are both dark haired and similarly olive-skinned, one a year or two older and leaner than the other, neither yet to hit their teens.

[*Me and my brother,*] he tells her. [*I'm the little chubby one.*]

The elder boy suddenly jumps up, two raised fists clenched in victory.

"You cheated!" says the younger.

"Don't be such a bad loser."

"I'll show you who's a loser."

And the ground shakes.

A rumble like thunder. But not.

More sounds, like Bonfire Night or New Year – thumps, bangs, whistles and whines – in turn followed by running, shouts, screams. Smoke rolls in like a fog, the memories becoming now confused, fragmented, breaking up into isolated snapshots, film-like clips, each playing on a loop, spaced out in the mindscape like the hilltop towns peeping out of the misty landscape, pulling her attention now here, now there: a burning, upturned car, a charred arm lolling out of its broken window; a fallen church spire laid broken across the street, its bell embedded into the front windows of a little bakery, the aroma of fresh bread mixing with the acrid smell of cordite; a woman clasping the trigger-finger arm of a patchwork soldier, pleading, wailing, as another man kneels before them; three tanks emerging in unruly formation over the horizon, spaced out like the haphazardly planted trees, their long shadows too snaking down the hills.

[*I think that's enough.*]

And suddenly they are back in the little antechamber, sitting in two chairs, facing each other.

[*Our only sin was to have what they didn't,*] he says.

She thinks of her own blanked-out or unremembered childhood – was it like that? Which is why he's showing her this, of course: to establish common ground, a basis for trust.

So what happened then? she asks.

[*Compliance did not ensure safety – we learned that, quickly and dearly. Some of us ran. Some lived for a time in the caves, up in the cliffs, places only the locals knew. We hunted, scavenged, stole. Eventually, we decided to make our way to the city. And there it was harder, in some ways; in other ways, easier. More danger, but more opportunity. After my brother disappeared, I decided to take my chances with the boats. Which weren't good. Though they were never short of customers. They'd pack so many in, some didn't even make it out to sea. Two weeks of shitting and pissing over the side, sleeping standing up, only what food you took with you. And most likely to be sunk by the sea drones. If you fell overboard, they left you. And still you'd get mothers who couldn't afford the passage begging strangers to take their children.*]

Mothers like hers? But that answer is closed to her, lying behind her own locked door, and to which she doesn't yet have the key.

He unfolds the rest of his story, one that could indeed have been hers: washed up with others fleeing the conflicts, snatched into one of the street dens, taught to thieve, to hack, his natural talent at some point spotted, trained, utilised, and from there graduating up the food chain, and eventually into the employ of people like Friedler.

Is that his name? she asks. *The man?*

He nods.

I don't like him.

He shrugs. [*What's to like?*]

Then how can you work for him? He's a scumbag.

[*You'll hear no counterargument from me.*]

What does he want me for?

[*What he wants everyone for: his own ends.*]

Which is what?

A pointless question, for she already suspects that she knows what that is, in broad outline at least, and he doesn't bother to answer.

Well, she says, *whatever it is, I won't do it.*

He nods again, as if acknowledging the wisdom of this.

[*If only that were an option,*] he replies.

And the room disappears.

SHE AWAKES some time later, disoriented and drained by her experience. The man in black is gone; in his place, sprawled across her bed, is Lily.

"Well this is a pickle, Squidge."

She is chewing at her fingers, worrying at a hangnail in that characteristic anxious-pensive fashion.

So what would you advise, phantom Lily? Alright for you, you're just a ... what? Half a daydream, half a memory, half an implant glitch – too many halves, but whatever she is, it's not much use to Squirrel.

And what *would* Lily do, in her position? Make the best of it. Make a plan. Use her skills, her nous. Make a bargain –

they *want* something, so make them work for it. Use it to find a way to get out.

When she next wakes there is food waiting for her; she picks at it – enough to sustain her, but not, she hopes, for the drugs to have full effect (though whether this strategy is working, who knows). She gets up and knocks on the fourth wall, which to her surprise doesn't feel like glass at all, but solidly wall-like.

"Hello? Hello!"

Eventually, the wall disappears, and the man in black is there, his glasses back in place.

"OK," she says. "Train me, then."

[*Do you promise not to misbehave?*]

"No," she replies, after some reflection. "But I do promise to listen."

He considers this.

"But I have two conditions," she adds.

He raises his eyebrows, just visible above the goggles. [*I don't think you're in a position to negotiate,*] he says, but nonetheless waits for her to continue.

"One: no more drugs." She points at the half-finished food. "And two: I want out of this." She gestures at her glass-fronted cage. "Right away."

The man nods thoughtfully, sighs, and turns and walks away.

The wall materialises back into place.

WHEN HE RETURNS a few hours later, there is a small drone hovering above his left shoulder, purring quietly, like a witch's familiar. It's about the size and shape of a large apple, its surface made of the same dark, unreflective material as his suit.

"What's that?"

[*Your new best friend,*] he says. [*In case you get lost. A chaperdrone!*]

And with that the glass wall opens – a door-shaped absence appearing in its seamless surface – and tentatively she steps through, her eyes and ears already sharpening in anticipation of new territory.

He leads her down the corridor, turning to smirk as she stalls before each cell, gawping at the neighbours she's never met but only heard.

"What are they?"

[*Experiments.*]

"Did Friedler do them all?"

[*Had someone else to. And if you want to ask me anything from now on, do it in camera.*]

"What?"

[*Privately, mind to mind. Didn't they teach you Latin in that brothel of yours?*]

Not a brothel. I was a thief. A streetsweep.

[*Not a distinction you need to take any pride in.*]

Just before the end of the corridor – where there is a large wooden door – he turns right, and they head down a flight of stone stairs and on through a maze of further twists and turns, past more closed doors.

So where is this? she asks.

[*Staff quarters.*]

Where?

[*Mayor's house.*]

She stops. "Wait, *that . . .*" – some basic arithmetic – "Friedler works for the *mayor*?"

The man in black stops too, turns, looks agitatedly from side to side, an annoyed frown.

[*Friedler* is *the mayor, you little imbecile.*] He shakes his head. [*That brothel madam really wants shooting.*]

THEY CHICANE through further twists of passageway – maybe he wasn't joking about her needing the drone-guide – down two more flights of steps and finally into a murky corridor with only one shabby looking door at the end.

God, what do they keep in there? she asks.

[*You.*] He smiles.

He opens the door and ushers her before him, the little drone in tow.

It's not much bigger than the glass cage she's just left, cold and dimly lit by a tattered old lamp, but at least there's a window, from which she can tell that it's night.

[*We'll begin the training tomorrow,*] he says, and goes to leave.

Wait. What do I call you? she asks. *Do you have a name?*

He pauses.

[*Yes,*] he says. [*Yes I do.*]

She waits. He does too.

Seriously? she says. *You're not going to tell me?*

[*Names are a form of power, a token of trust. Find out someone's name, you can know all sorts of things about them – their history, their location, their genealogy. If you're a good girl, one day I'll tell you yours.*]

She frowns, but is immediately distracted as something large swims by the window.

[*I trust you packed your snorkel?*] He smiles again. [*Goodnight.*]

He leaves, closing the door behind him.

CHAPTER TWO

"AND HOW IS SHE TODAY?" he asks.

[*Still reacclimatising,*] Azimuth replies, [*but stabilising well.*]

Caulden toys with the pen on his desk – not actually his pen, of course, and not his desk either. Pointless, really – both the digital replica and the original. For when did he last write anything by hand?

At least the girl seems to be mentally intact – relatively speaking.

Using the original was an enormous risk. They could have lost her completely. Faced with the truth at the end of the game, she might have rejected it, retreated into the fictional persona and refused to re-emerge into reality – well, perhaps that word should have scare quotes. Or, she might simply have gone insane – again. Either way, they'd have a hard time finding another one as powerful. But what could he do? They had to try something. The balcony was the last straw, a straw that had come within a hair's breadth of exposing everything – and *that* not for the first time either. But Azimuth's hypothesis had proven correct: the immersion *had* been greater.

"So it worked, we think?"

[*Too early to say, I'm afraid. The most subtle and profound forms of suggestion can take time to bear fruit. We shall have to wait and see.*]

Like a tree. You plant the seed, you water it, feed it, and you wait. Or in this case, you drug it with behaviourally modifying chemicals, bombard it with subliminal suggestions, and *then* you wait. They'd had to sail very close to the wind to embed just the right message. After all, the best lies are as near as possible to the truth. Which was a tricky thing to pull off. The script had to be dynamic and open-ended enough for her to feel that she was making her own decisions, her own discoveries, and yet still allow her to be led where they wanted her to go (with Azimuth adapting and directing things on the fly). And even then, she had resisted. The vampire thing! The creepy ritual! What the hell was all *that* about? *That* wasn't in the script.

[*Her unconscious resistance colouring the experience,*] Azimuth suggests. [*She had obviously started to distrust the scenario from early on.*]

As in a dream. Her rational mind trying to make sense of the experiences they were feeding her, reshaping them in the process, retelling the story in her own genre – which was nineteenth-century Gothic horror fiction, apparently. Her reading list has a lot to answer for. But the whole thing had been surprisingly coherent and stable – if a little weird.

And she *had* been tempted, hadn't she? Even though, ultimately, she had declined the Marquise's offer, which had "lost" her the "game". A shame.

Still, a step closer. They will see if this drugged-up tree bears fruit, or whether they'll have to go back to planting saplings.

He likes that line, though. What was it? *The drones just need a queen!* Yes! Perfect. Where did that come from?

[*It seemed apposite.*]

Yes, very apt. From the princess in the tower to the queen of the hive.

Which is what they need her to be, of course, if this is all to work out.

To Caulden's annoyance, the pen he's been fiddling with has broken, and virtual ink is now smeared over his virtual desk and all over his virtual fingers. What is the point in this level of realism?

"Let's see how it all plays out," he says. "As long as it plays out quickly."

"SO THEY KNEW what would happen?" Eva asks.

[*To an extent,*] Azimuth admits.

"But they had an opportunity? To change the way things would go?"

[*It was more complicated than that. There were numerous contributory factors, countless variables. The correct path may not have been clear to them.*]

And they didn't take it.

This is what has obsessed her ever since the end of the game. She has never really questioned her present, has always seen the way the world is now as being in some way inevitable. The unavoidable outcome of an unalterable sequence of events, the fixed effect of previously fixed causes. But now, she sees that this is not necessarily the case.

Of course, this is the central lesson of *Sabotage*: Things need not have been as they are! There are counterfactual worlds, roads not taken, cruxes at which one path was chosen rather than another, one event happened and another did not. Worlds where the October Revolution was delayed – until November, say, or brought forward to July; or where the tsarist regime never fell at all. But – strangely, now she thinks about it – Eva had not thought to apply this simple fundamental principle to the world *as it is now*; to *her own* world. It is only in playing this more recently set game – the most recent setting of *Sabotage* yet – that the point has become obvious. There had been a tipping or a turning point, an opportunity to avoid what has already now happened; and they did not take it.

"Can we play again?"

[*Maybe another day? You need your rest.*]

She is not surprised by this response. They are afraid – Azimuth and her father – worried she might not come back out this time. And maybe she is too, a little; because maybe there's also some part of her that *wants* that. She had gone in too deep, had even forgotten that she was playing; had lost herself; had lost her *self*. And in that forgetting, that amnesiac immersion, had come a delirious freedom.

But it was curious, why that had happened. There are always certain things that *Sabotage* will give you – qualities, personal characteristics. Alex was far more confident than Eva is; the way she is with men, her courage, her cunning and resourcefulness, her unwavering determination. She wishes she could be more like that. But the game could also gift you actual knowledge – theoretical, factual. You knew things, while playing, that you did not know before; even abilities and experiences. Which is why it can be so easy to lose yourself, of course, to become someone else. But all these gifts are usually *in addition to*, not *instead of*, and this is the first time *Sabotage* had taken something *away*: knowledge of who she truly is. That she is aware of, anyway.

And of course, that lovely self-forgetful immersion is a double-edged thing. For if it is possible to think of *there* as real, then who is to say, sitting here now in this room at this window, staring out at those pale distant hills, that *this* is not the dream, and Château de Lefatigué the reality? Or that *both* are in fact unreal?

[*It does not pay to entertain such radical scepticism. It is corrosive.*]

"I'm not paid to entertain *anything*, that I'm aware of."

[*There is no need for flippancy. The point is a serious one.*]

Touchy. Still worried about her mental imbalance, evidently.

"So was Alex a real person?" she asks.

[*Define "real".*]

Evasive.

"Well, what about The Society?"

[*You may look up these questions for yourself, you know.*]

"Charlotte de Lefatigué?"

[*I refer the honourable lady to the answer I gave some moments ago.*]

But looking things up would be tantamount to asking Azimuth, for it would only filter what she is allowed to see anyway; even *change* it, possibly. Probably.

On balance, Eva decides that Alex was real – at least, she *felt* real. But what does that even mean? A convincing backstory? A coherent personality? Having goals and motivations and desires? Well, she was certainly very driven: she cared about what she wanted to achieve, enough even to risk her own life. And as for personality, well, she had that in spades: humour, cynicism, sass, compassion, even regret. But most of all, she had *interiority*. There was something *it was like* to *be* Alex, something – Eva feels – genuine. It is when you stepped out of that, into her backstory, that things began to go a bit wonky – the whole "Society of the Invisible Hand" thing! Like some pulpy homage to something out of Sherlock Holmes (if Moriarty had been a gay vampire – hmm, not canon, but who knows . . .).

And as for Château de Lefatigué, well, apart from the obvious (*le fatigué,* "the tired one" – not an unfitting epithet for an energy-sapping vampire who must get her sustenance from preying on men), the whole supernatural element made it read more like a ghost story than a genuine historical scenario; almost as if Eva was live role-playing a parable or a fable.

But aside from creaky backstory and implausible plotting, there was something else that had unsettled her. Of course, the Marquise was right: what history had done to women, the effect of this gender imbalance on our view of nature, the environment, of ourselves and each other. But it was what Charlotte de Lefatigué had chosen to *do* with her power, how she sought to redress that imbalance – to "utilise" men, as she had put it, even if this were mere metaphor (not to drain their vital essence for her eternal youth, but to use it to reshape the world in her own image; in the *Goddess's* image). But how was that any better? Shouldn't there be gods *as well as* goddesses? A harmony in Heaven?

Which is why, perhaps, at some instinctual level, she had rejected Charlotte's offer, had refused to "take over" from her (whatever that would have entailed – the logistics of which seem shakier the more she thinks about it); and which had lost her the game, ultimately, allowing "Savvy" (Azimuth) to scupper Alex's plans to expose The Society.

. . . But if Savvy was Azimuth, she's been sleeping with the AI.

Eurgh.

Has this happened before?

Nothing to say on that, Azimuth?

But in a sense, *everyone* in the game is the AI – like Dracula and his "servants"! A one-man show, playing every part – Savvy, the Marquise, little well-mannered Herr Gruber, even Alex herself (to an extent). And the castle, the labyrinth, from the snow bowing down the pine-needled trees to the heavy red-blue tapestries swaying in the draughty great hall.

It was all Azimuth: just part of the same dumb, blind, insentient system.

[*Gee, thanks.*]

And all of which, without Eva to imbue it with meaning and significance, with *real* feeling and *real* life, had no inherent *reality* at all. For Azimuth has no desires or dreams or pleasures or regrets; only Eva has those, creating her own puppet theatre out of patterns in the data.

And so really, if anything, she'd been sleeping with herself.

[*I feel like I've been deconstructed.*]

"What's the matter? Don't like the taste of your own medicine?"

Not that she would *not* like to be a queen. In fact, she thinks she'd make a pretty good ruler. Strong and wise. Compassionate and merciful. Dispensing justice and ensuring peace. Overseeing a renaissance of literature and the arts! But Charlotte was not that sort of sovereign; she was . . . singular, cold, virginal, sterile. An object of formal veneration, an emblem of frigid power, but not . . . *fruitful*. No, if ever she had the chance, Eva would be far different from that. There would be parties! Balls and dancing! Feasts! Courtly flirtation and dalliance! (Is that where "courting" comes from? The courtly behaviour of courtiers at Court?)

[*Yes, "courting", in the popular sense of a romantic involvement with a view to marriage, derives ultimately from the sort of mannered behaviour expected of courtiers vying for royal favour.*]

Why can't she play games like *that*? Fin-de-siècle France? Marie Antoinette! Versailles! But that, unfortunately, has not yet been a setting for *Sabotage*. Could it be?

[*We could look into it.*]

She looks again out the window, out at the hills, and back onto the inner balcony, with its little red forbidding light. She doesn't like that view – the view down, through the arcology's central shaft; she doesn't know why. Perhaps it's what it reminds her of: the night, and the voices that night-time brings.

CAULDEN HAD WANTED to see the silver city again – that shining place of futuristic promise, glimpsed only from afar on that first and so far only sighting – to see it up close, to walk its streets, to meet its people. But his second visit had been to somewhere else entirely.

[*The Hall of Remembering,*] the tall figure had informed him, that same bone-voice reverberating at the back of his skull and down the length of his spine.

It was indeed a hall, though whether museum or mausoleum, Caulden hadn't been quite sure – still isn't. It was dedicated to row upon row of enormous statues – exquisite, intricate, disquieting, grotesque – each one drained of living colour, but animated in a slow dance, each limb moving to a funereal beat with a sort of mournful pomp. Nothing Caulden witnessed then or since has been entirely free of this underlying gloominess. They have built incredible things, achieved incredible things – both organic and inorganic, songs of flesh as well as stone and steel. But there is an unassuageable melancholy about all that they have done, as if each creation were birthed deep in the shadow of some fatalistic pessimism. And so whatever beauty or magnificence their creations evoked, there was always some facet that marred or offset it, that both undermined and questioned its worth.

A case in point: he had stopped before an enormous figure of … well, he could not say "man", in good conscience, or even *humanoid*, but let that word suffice. The figure was grappling with some serpent-like thing, its finely toned muscles straining in athletic exertion as it struggled to best the creature – a Hercules fighting an Achelous – but which, on closer inspection, revealed itself to be part of the figure itself, emerging from it like a tail that split into many Hydra-like heads, each of which it ineffectually attempted to fend off, to deter from feasting on its own flesh; a self-cannibalistic hybrid.

Most disquietingly of all, he could not decide whether or not the statue was alive.

[*There comes a point where that question is not so simply answered,*] the creature had replied, in response to his unvoiced quandary. [*We do not share the same distinctions as you – between the natural and the artificial, the living and the inanimate.*]

But there were other statues, each as graphic, even *more* challenging, that verged upon the obscene, the horrific.

"What are they for?" Caulden had asked eventually.

[*As the hall's name suggests, they are reminders.*]

"Of what?"

[*That all our endeavours are ultimately futile.*]

They were memento mori. Premeditations of the evils that all flesh is heir to. Not an uncommon theme in our own art, religion and philosophy: time devours all things. But here was a slightly different message, or one taken to its absurd conclusion; one where the enemy was not time, but the false hope of any ambition, any undertaking at all. It was as if the enemy were life itself.

[*Tempus edax rerum,*] the figure noted, approvingly, as if reading his thoughts – which, of course, it had been; like Azimuth, but not. [*Ovid, quoting Pythagoras. Time devours all things. And so you see, it is in the nature of life to destroy itself. For are not all creatures also the agents of time?*]

For beings from another world, they are impressively knowledgeable about human culture.

But it is their technology that has been most impressive. So far beyond his understanding as to verge upon the magical. They have conquered Nature. And this is what confuses him: why that knowledge and power should be a cause for such morbidity. For Caulden, science has always been the great liberator, the source of eternal optimism, a reason *not* to be fatalistic or pessimistic. For whatever problem is faced, there will be – maybe not now, maybe only at the end of a long path of struggle and frustration – a way. But such knowledge and power seem only to have made them dismal.

One time, at his expression of wonder at some technological marvel, the creature had taken him to task.

[*You focus always on our feats of engineering, but you ignore the social and the political, the spiritual. These are equally, if not more important achievements.*]

But it is this – the cultural aspect – that he most struggles with; that makes him hope that what they are trying to teach him – the science that he is attempting to reverse engineer – can be disentangled from their worldview, that it is not in some inextricable way imbued with their values and norms. He tries to hide his reactions to all this, not always successfully. But the creature is forgiving of his queasiness, accommodating of his culture shock. Still, it is hard. Nature, however weird and strange, is somehow easier to accept than even the most modest deviations from the norms of nurture. That said, their natural world was disquieting enough.

Another time, he had found himself stood on some sort of viewing platform or form of transport, floating soundlessly over a ruddy landscape that reminded him in certain respects of a red-rock Arizona canyon or Australian outback.

[*These are what we call the Deadlands.*]

And indeed it did look as if nothing could survive there – not from heat, but the lack of it.

A peculiar look overcame the creature's face. [*Watch,*] it said, pointed to a jagged outcrop of red stone, and clapped twice; the noise echoed slow and dull across the desolate landscape – was the atmosphere thinner there? – and an enormous flying creature – somewhere in shape between bat and vulture, but of immensely greater size – lifted off, detaching itself from the stone perch with which it had blended, so artfully that it was as if part of the rock itself was taking flight.

The eerie safari had continued and, to his diminishing relish, other mammoth and stealthy entities had been pointed out to him.

He felt both sickened and mesmerised. And puzzled: that life there had become so gigantic, so patient and slothlike – the adaptive qualities forced on extremophiles by the environment, he supposed – but it was almost as if evolution had given up, had pruned its own developmental tree, resorting to earlier, more primitive and fundamental expressions.

When night fell, the temperature dropped even further, but paradoxically things had begun to liven up. The muffled, unidentifiable calls – deep resonant moans, pitiful whines – accompanied by a procession of torpid forms, each barely registering on the creature's thermal-vision screen. Evidently, life went on.

But it was not at its best.

CHAPTER THREE

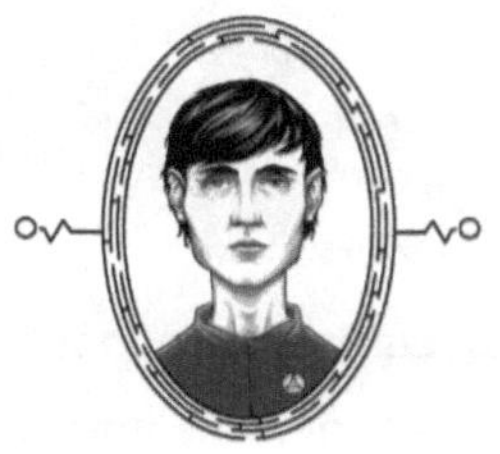

A HIGH-PITCHED SOUND swoops down through the oc-
taves, warbling through the water, before rising again; like a
theremin.

And with it the darkness begins to unknit.

Once again: a keening, almost plaintive, followed by a
cackling trail of clicks.

And there is light; dim, occluded at first, wavering as
shifting forms flash and swirl before it, but growing now,
getting brighter.

And a third time: the same soupy swooping and chittering.

And the light now is clear, unobscured . . . but already
starting to fade; for everything now is fading, a deeper black-
ness seeping in from the periphery of his vision, shrinking
it to a monochrome vignette.

Is this dying?

He is vaguely, apathetically aware that his limbs have
stopped their thrashing.

Strange suddenly how quiet it is, how peaceful; the cold almost lulling.

A single black form appears, a speck in the eye, its blurry silhouette eroded by the dimming light.

Ah, Percy thinks. *Come to deliver the coup de grâce.*

THE SILHOUETTE kneels over him, panting.

Percy retches again – more bile and water – and continues to cough, each spasm constricting a band across his temples.

He is back on the boat – but no, not the water taxi; some other craft, sleek and stealthy black.

The figure removes one dark glove and reaches over, laying a surprisingly warm hand on the side of his neck for a few beats. "You'll live," it says eventually – a female voice. "No thanks to you."

The woman gets up – for he can confirm now the definitive outline of her form – and half-stands, hands on knees, still winded from her exertions. She turns to face him; she is wearing a pair of goggles, some sort of visor, which she removes from her eyes and lets fall on a band about her neck, before pulling back a hood that is attached to the body of her outfit. It is some sort of wetsuit, though of a strange substance – similar, in fact, to something that he's seen, and recently. Where was that? The pulsing band of pain won't allow him to remember.

But her face: *that* he remembers.

"Not-Antonio," she says, shaking her head, her breathing finally slowing. "Don't you know what's not good for you?"

"WE'RE ALMOST THERE."

Wherever *there* is takes them out into the lagoon, as she pilots the boat between the half-submerged remnants of the old city, away from the Arc and the dwindling urban hub that clusters limpet-like wretchedly about its hillside. His coughing is lessening and he has stopped throwing up, but he is feeble as a newborn, body *and* mind, numbed by the soaking fog through which they still move, as if it has permeated more than just his clothes.

"What were those things?"

"Lorelei. Loreleis?" A quizzical look, pondering a moment the correct plural form, and she shrugs. "Somebody's little science experiment gone rogue. Whoever made them also forgot to neuter them, so for the last few years they've been spreading along the coast. Not seen them so aggressive, though. Seemed to take a particular shine to you."

Friedler's mermaids.

"Did you . . . When I was in the water, how did you—"

"Killer whale calls. Handy. Scares away most things. Lorelei have been spliced from salmon DNA, we think, which is what orcas mostly live on, so it's natural it should work on them."

We?

The subdued outlines of the wrecks of buildings phase in and out through the shifting fog – just like his thoughts.

"Where are we going?"

"The old maritime museum, just down from where the marina used to be."

For now, of course, everywhere is marina.

"Why there?"

"You judging my postcode?" She grins, which fades to a look of concern; and then that fades too, along with every-thing else.

THERE IS SINGING. A high, female voice, wordless. Percy's eyes track the sound to a shape stood at a counter, its outline bleared against a set of murky windows filtering in the dim light some yards to his right, the clatter of cups and bowls, the steely rattle of cutlery, cooking aromas, steam.

It is a large, high space, sporadically lit, cable lights strewn about like Christmas decorations, hung up in corners and draped over pipes and girders. Podia dot the polished wooden floor, some still hosting their original glass cases, one or two even intact, housing models of ships, collections of scrimshaw, damp-mottled navigation charts, and other maritime memorabilia. Fittingly, the whole floor is on a slight tilt – unless he is.

His headache has lessened, but not disappeared, and as he tries to sit up, hinges and springs creaking rustily beneath him as he shifts – some sort of camp bed? – he is quickly dissuaded by a sharp stab in his chest, and slumps back.

There is a slight pressure on his left arm. He raises it, pushing back a white sleeve of some sort of gown to discover a small glowing-red box, pulsing in and out with a mysterious internal effort. Reflexively he scans the room and discovers, to his left, his clothes and boots drying on a rack next to a little old-fashioned heater.

"Ah, good." The singing has stopped, and the singer – Cherri, or whoever she is – has turned and is now moving toward him, bearing two steaming bowls of something that smells like its from one of Market Square's food stalls, a spoon sticking out from each. "Sorry about the attire," she nods at the gown. "All we had. So how are you feeling now?"

"Like I've been run over."

"That'll pass. Here." She hands him a bowl. "Careful, it's hot."

"What's this?" He indicates the box on his arm.

"Re-oxygenating your blood."

"Right. And where are we?"

"The old maritime museum, as I told you."

"How . . ." But whatever he was going to have asked, his brain has decided not to tell him.

"Don't worry," she says. "It'll come back." Meaning, presumably, his ability to hold a coherent thought.

She clears some salty bric-a-brac off a little upturned packing case, drags it to one side of the bed, sits down on it and begins blowing on and sipping her soup.

"Come on, eat. You have questions, I know. But you'll have to be patient. And there's a lot to unpack."

He raises a spoonful, blows on it, and takes a dutiful sip: fish stew. And the association kills his appetite dead. He sets it down on the floor beside the camp bed.

She is no longer in the black wetsuit type thing, but jeans, trainers and a fittingly nautical thick-ribbed jumper. Her long black hair is tied back in a pony tail. The only carry-over from her "professional" outfit is the single red-stoned ring on her right hand.

"And 'Cherri'?" he finally manages.

She gives a mock-guilty smile. "Sorry about that. Name's Abi. Even once I worked out what you were, didn't know if I could trust you."

"And you can now?"

She shrugs and tilts her head: *We'll see, won't we?*

"So who are you?" he asks. "I mean, if you're not a . . . you know."

She laughs.

"Well, there's not a short answer to that." She sets down her bowl. "Are you lying comfortably?"

"THAT GIRL you showed me – the picture," Abi begins. "She was my sister."

"I . . . I'm sorry. If I'd have known that, I'd—"

"Well, as I say, *was* my sister. What she is now, God knows."

She picks up her bowl again, but just stirs the contents with her spoon and stares into the homemade whirlpool, before continuing. She'd always known Eva was different. Talking to herself, having conversations with the air, laughing at jokes no one else had heard. But it was mostly harmless, eccentricities. Give her an object, a ring, a book or a shoe, and she would tell you its story, where it had come from, who'd owned it. Just childish fun, Abi had thought, make-believe. But there was other, weirder stuff, things she couldn't know – what people were thinking or feeling, things that were going to happen. And so Abi had eventually convinced herself that Eva was a Natural. Hard, Percy realises, with mental illness, especially with those close to us; we prefer to make excuses for their behaviour than accept the hard truth.

Some of this must have been betrayed on his face, for she stops.

"What?"

"Oh, I don't . . . Naturals aren't a real thing," he says. "I mean, no offence, but I'm certain there are other explanations."

She snorts. "Well, who am *I* to question your certainty?" She stirs her bowl some more.

The girl was also precocious – "Brighter than I am, and I'm no slouch" – always reading, always talking and thinking about things – history, mythology, science, books and films – her magpie brain a curiosity shop of intellectual bric-a-brac. But in other ways she was unworldly, gullible. Abi had tried to protect her, from people that would take advantage of that naivety, but she'd been little more than a kid herself, with her own stuff going on – "Which I won't bore you with" – and at some point after Eva had just turned sixteen, the girl had just vanished.

From there on it is the type of story with which Percy is all too familiar. The sisters had only had each other – the mother absent, run off some years before; the father, whom she'd had good reason to run off from, a useless Hazer. And the teachers, the authorities, either apathetic or patronising, telling her not to worry, that people go missing all the time. "She's probably just staying with a friend, love." But she had no friends. And she'd never go anywhere without telling her sister.

At first she'd thought it was sex traffickers. As the pathologist's facial reconstruction had suggested, she was a good looking girl. But when Abi had made the connection with Naturals, and that there was a market for them, it had all fallen into place.

"Someone had seen what she was, and they'd nabbed her."

Abi had followed what trails she could find, which had eventually brought her south. Being good with tech, she'd managed to find work in one of the hack-shacks, which got her contacts she could use, taught her new skills, how to hack the face-rec databases, the inventories for the black markets. But there was nothing. It was as if the girl never existed. Her life had been wiped.

"Someone must have done that," she says. "Someone with the power to."

She puts her soup down again and rubs her hands to warm them, staring into the unlit corners of the large space.

And then she had found her.

It was from the municipal street camera network, flagged by a face-rec algorithm she'd had running on the dark web marketplaces, footage some degenerate had lucked upon – "If that's the word" – and was trying to sell. Resolution wasn't great, but she'd managed to clean it up: it was definitely her.

"Maybe she'd escaped from whoever'd had her, then decided she'd had enough. But anyway, she'd jumped from the old bridge down on Union Street."

"When was this?" he asks.

"A year or so ago. No other record of it. No crime scene report, nothing in the Feeds. Again, like it never happened." She takes the bobble out of her hair, shakes it loose and reties it, and sits picking at her nails. "I thought about going back home. Wherever she'd been, whoever'd taken her, I wasn't going to get justice or change anything. You've seen this place, right? Founders Way? The clubs? That's just the tip of it. Like fighting the tide." Her brow knits and her mouth tightens into a line. "But just as I was about to head off, I saw her again."

She gets up, takes her half-finished bowl back to the sink, walks over to the little heater and turns it up a notch, and comes to sit back down on the crate.

"I'd gotten in with the street girls by then, figured it was the best way to find out if any of the johns had seen her."

"So, do you actually … you know … do you … with the …"

"Fuck them?" She laughs. "Jesus, Antonio, your diction is practically Victorian."

"So that night, when we—"

"Relax, Galahad. Your holy grail would have been safe with me. I'd have knocked you out with something in my little box of tricks, hacked your implant, rifled through your memories, then left you with some of my own. You'd have woken up next morning none the wiser, just a hazy memory of having had a really lovely time.

"Anyway, as I say, suddenly there she is, in this john's memories – an Arc resident – his *recent* memories, mind you; like, the week before. Just a glimpse; a view of her on a balcony. But she was alive. How can that be, I thought? And then it clicked – what they'd done."

Percy nods. He tells her about the autopsy, the pathologist's report, about the one-year-old adult virgin.

"But why?" she says. "That's what I don't get. I mean, doesn't look like it's for sex dolls. To make more Naturals? Would that even work?"

"You're asking the wrong sceptic, I'm afraid."

"Well, just because *you* don't believe, doesn't mean *they* don't."

He coughs, which triggers a few more. He leans back, panting.

"Right," she says, frowning, "we should check on your blood oxygen, shouldn't we?", reaching across to tap a few times on his wrist device, which elicits a comforting series of chirrups and cheeps. "OK, almost there. How's your chest, now?"

He tests the muscles with the palm of his hand. "Sore."

"CPR." A smile of mock apology. "My bad."

"It was lucky you were there," he says.

Her eyes briefly meet his and she looks quickly away. "Get some more sleep." She stands to reach over and plump up the pillows behind his head, gathers the blankets and lifts them up better to cover him.

"Why *were* you there?" he asks.

"Hmm?"

"How did you know I was in trouble? Where I'd be?"

"Got lucky, I guess — lucky for you, anyway. You really should get some more rest."

There is a creak of a door and they both turn as a man enters.

The man in black.

CHAPTER FOUR

"DON'T THINK MUCH of your view, Squidge."

Lily is back again, stood with her arms folded, rocking back and fore on one high heel as she stares out the window. Is it a window, if it's underwater? A porthole, then? Or do those have to be round? Lily's visits are increasing in frequency, for whatever reason. Stress, maybe; a psychic release valve. "God, I hope this glass is reinforced, or something." She taps soundlessly upon it with a phantom knuckle. "*That's* a wakeup call you don't want." She rubs her upper arms. "Like the bloody North Pole in here."

"Didn't think ghosts could feel cold," Squirrel says.

"Colder than a polar bear's ballsack. You should demand an upgrade." She turns back to half-face Squirrel – she never quite meets her eyes, never unequivocally answers her questions, like she exists at a tangent to everything. Maybe that's what death is. A thoughtful finger taps her chin. "Or is that where the penguins are?" She raises the finger to correct herself. "*Were.*"

"You know, you could actually suggest something useful."

But Lily just turns back and continues gazing out the window, tilting her head now and then as if spying something ominous in the murky depths outside.

But she's right, on all counts: peeling wallpaper, damp; a punitively small bed; a bathroom so tiny it's little more than a closet with a toilet and a sink; an old rickety plastic chair; a warped bamboo bedside cabinet, with a door that won't open, hosting a lamp with a tawdry, tasselled shade; and no source of heat anywhere.

Her only company is the chaperdrone, a near-silent sentinel, hovering in the corner of the room with a barely audible hum.

"Tell whatshisface I'm freezing to death," Squirrel says to it, and as with every other time so far, receives no response. In fact, it only acknowledges her existence whenever she goes near the door, at which point it will move in front to bar any attempt at exit. Does that mean it's not locked?

She should have brought the tablet with her, if only she'd thought of it, then at least she could watch or read or play something. And she's starting to get hungry. And her arm and leg and eye socket are beginning to ache. At least in her glass-fronted cage she had medication, food, warmth and private bot-care.

How long does he plan to keep her here?

I need food and heat and drugs! she sends out into the void.

[*You only had to ask,*] the void's instantaneous reply.

The fucker. Like a lab rat, only rewarded when her random actions hit upon the required response.

I don't think much of your teaching style.

[*I've already told you: all communication in camera. That includes room service.*]

A while later the door opens – no knock ("I could've been changing!" in mock indignation) – and a diminutive robot trundles in carrying an ancient looking heater and a little plastic snack box, like a little kid's, which she supposes is better than nothing.

What about drugs?

[*Pain is good for focus, remember? Don't want you forming a habit.*]

She eyes the snack box warily.

So what now?

[*You're cranky. Get some sleep.*]

The snack box contains a cheese sandwich, an apple and a carton of blackcurrant squash, as well as some basic toiletries. She wolfs her food, cleans her teeth, gets into bed and switches off the lamp, shivering under the meagre duvet as her eyes adjust to the darkness . . . and the swirling half-formed shapes outside the window.

Can I get some curtains?

[*No.*]

SHE AWAKES to an intermittent buzzing and a little melody rising steadily in volume. It's an alarm call, courtesy of the drone. How sweet. Perhaps it also makes tea.

"What time is it?"

No response from the drone. She sighs and tries again.

What time is it?

[*Time to get up. See you in ten.*]

My mind or yours?

[*Follow the drone.*]

The heater has been going all night, which together with her breath has produced a white fog on the window and dripping rivulets of moisture down the walls. A change of clothes awaits her on the rickety chair, and on the bedside cabinet, her snack box has been replenished with some sort of yellow fruit, a packet of crisps, and even a cup of tea (so that's that question answered, perhaps).

She tries the fruit first, biting into its thick, rubbery rind, before realising it must be peeled apart to reveal the soft pale flesh inside. It tastes slightly waxy.

What's the yellow thing?

[*My God, you've never eaten a banana?*]

Have you got anything else?

[*So ungrateful. They're like hen's teeth.*]

I don't think I like them.

[*Do you like starving?*]

She sips the tea.

There's no sugar in this. Could I have coffee?

No response.

She follows the chaperdrone out the door and through the maze of passageways, along the corridors with their rows of branching doors, all closed.

What happened to all the servants?

[*They asked too many questions.*]

Seriously, where are they?

[*I see now why that Denton oaf was so keen to get rid of you.*]

At mention of his name, Squirrel experiences a reflexive choke of anxiety.

[*Interesting. . .*] observes the stranger in her head.

THE DRONE EVENTUALLY deposits her into a spacious hallway, lit from above by a giant chandelier like a UFO from some old film, and on the walls by bracketed lamps, the light from all of which is multiplied by several large gold-framed mirrors. There is a set of imposing wooden doors in front of her, and in front of them, the man in black, back in his customary guise.

[*You slept well?*] he asks.

Like a baby. A freezing baby, anyway. That heater is rubbish.

[*Well you got the baby bit right. So stop being one. A bit of cold is about to be the least of your worries.*]

Which has the desired effect of shutting up her whining.

He moves toward the main doors and opens another smaller door set within the one on the right, ushering her through it as the drone follows close behind. But when they emerge it is night-time, a cloudless black and star-spangled sky – she had assumed it would be day, that what she'd just had was breakfast (if you could call it that) – and feels suddenly disconcerted.

[*Behold!*] he says with a flamboyant flourish of his hands. [*The mayoral gardens.*]

They are stood at the top of a set of broad stone steps that lead down and through pristinely ordered patches of shrubbery, a range of well-trained and exotic-looking trees, lawns bordered by neatly tended flower beds, and all contained within a high stone bounding wall.

[*He's not green fingered himself, but employs those who are, so that others may think of him as having an interest.*]

Why should I care?

[*Because personality is free information. You never know when it may come in handy.*]

As they walk she turns her head to look back and up at the stolidly impressive house, rising six storeys above her (and, she now knows, descending a good few beneath as well). So this is what money and power buys you.

The man in black looks her way and smirks, but says nothing.

They reach a sizeable pair of wrought-iron gates, which move silently apart as they approach, and they step out onto the jetty – and the weather changes, the clear night now sodden with mist and fine drizzle.

She turns to him, frowning.

[*No,*] he says, [this *is what money and power buys you.*]

A LITTLE BOAT AWAITS, which two silent heavies, stood sentry at the gates, help them to board.

So where are we going?

[*Your old hunting ground. Market Square.*]

Why?

[Have you somewhere else you need to be?]

But why there?

[Because it'll be full of people whose minds will be on some-thing else.]

You want me to sweep *them? Why?*

His head points his black-windowed stare her way, the fog lamps along the canal glinting dimly off the lenses in lieu of pupils, and she shuts up.

Despite the weather, Market Square is, as he'd predicted, quite busy; an archetypal Saturday night, and all the archetypes are here. Gaggles of girls tottering by arm in arm, wearing far less than the elements demand, banter with braying blokes in short-sleeved shirts and beer coats, making their way to and from the clubs on Founders Way. The homeless, cocooned for the evening in ratty sleeping bags, hole up in cardboard forts, or sit tailor-fashion in clothes far from the latest cut. The food stalls plying a pungent, steaming trade, administer too late their stomach-lining carbohydrates. Jugglers and entertainers, their human or mechanical limbs daubed with fluorescent paint, vie with buskers of all musical stripes. Pedlars, of drugs or themselves, propositioning from the fringes, cast their loaded glances like lures into the flowing crowds.

So what's the plan? she asks.

[Sweep!]

She checks her implant, but it's still offline – whatever they've done to disable it is still in effect.

And how am I meant to do that?

[*Use your new-found skills. Show me what you can do.*]

He walks off and disappears immediately into the crowd.

Another test; it's the Bouts all over again.

And what am I looking for?

[*Surprise me.*]

She wishes she had her own stealth suit, or at least her own say in terms of wardrobe, feeling conspicuous in the too-clean, too-new jeans, the too-big t-shirt and jacket, all looking fresh off the shelf of some bargain retail outlet.

[*Invisibility is mostly in the mind,*] he tells her. [*Just act like no one's interested in you and you're not important. It's the role you've trained your whole life to play.*]

She begins to work the crowd.

First she falls into step behind a group of girls. But it's hard. How do you catch someone's eye without catching someone's eye?

"Can I help you, love?"

She looks hurriedly away and tries someone else, a man serving at one of the food stalls.

"What'll you have?"

Why isn't this working? She's looking them right in the eyes.

[*Then maybe it's not the eyes. . .*]

She thinks back over the times that it's happened: Denton, the man at the book stall, the giant, times with Lily and others back at the Den. There hadn't always been a locking of eyes — had there? But if it's something else, then what?

And he is beside her again, as is the drone, materialising out of the ether.

[*It's like watching Bambi learning to play chess.*]

THEY STROLL AROUND the periphery of the square, skirting the fringe of the crowds.

[*You're thinking of this like a thief would,*] the man in black tells her, [*or a hacker.*]

But isn't that what we're doing? Squirrel counters. Hacking someone's mind? Stealing their thoughts?

[*Yes – and no. It's true that a mind is networkable, just like an implant is. And that's its vulnerability. It's just a different sort of network, connected in a different way, and therefore accessed with a different set of keys. But most minds have no firewalls or passwords, no locks or bolts, because most people don't believe in mind reading; they think they already have mental privacy, simply by virtue of its being their mind. But it's not. And that notion of privacy disappears the moment you realise that the mind is something other than you think it is.*]

What?

[*A part of something bigger.*]

I don't understand.

He sighs. They wander over to a square-side bench, and he gestures for her to sit beside him.

[*Look.*]

He indicates one of the figures huddled in a shop doorway underneath layers of blankets and cardboard.

[*You currently think of that man's mind as being "over there", and that somehow you have to break into it, like it's a house.*

But that's not the case. The house is everywhere, and it doesn't just belong to him. Observe.]

And suddenly the crowds have disappeared and they are walking down a terraced street.

Where are we? she asks.

[*Wrong question. Not a "where" – at least, not in the sense you think. It's more of a "who". Namely, the man who's dreaming it.*]

They stop before a house distinguished from its neighbours by the fact of its being completely derelict: a caved-in roof, the upper floor a nest of broken timbers, the remaining windows smashed or boarded up. Inside is much the same: broken furniture, discarded children's toys, single shoes, dirty bowls and plates caked with scraps of decaying food, cracked picture frames and other household bric-a-brac, strewn about like the domestic survivors of a hurricane or a rocket strike.

So this is his *dream?*

[*This is his* self.] He picks a dusty framed photo off the mantlepiece that depicts a family of four: a man, woman, and two young girls, beaming back at the camera on a sunny day in the park. [*Houses are symbols of the self. In the physical world, each house is connected to its neighbour – shared walls and boundaries, drains, electricity, water supply. The same is true here.*]

They continue on, through the bomb site of a kitchen, and out into the garden; and there is the man himself, hammer in hand, trying to mend a broken fence.

[*So it would be more accurate to say that this is his part of a bigger dream. A little bit he has co-opted as his own, a smallholding. Like pioneers in the Wild West, staking out a claim on "common land". A claim to which he is similarly untitled.*]

What's the Wild West?

[Good grief.]

It's not just the fence that needs fixing; the garden itself is in disarray – a lawn choked with weeds and wildflowers; a little wooden shed with begrimed windows, the felt roof torn and tattered, its interior piled high with junk, the door hanging off its hinges.

So why is everything broken? If it's his dream, why doesn't he just dream whatever he wants?

[Do you? Dream whatever you want? A broken man dreams broken dreams – or rather, they dream him. Whatever pressures have brought him to this pass are psychic as well as material – depression, anxiety, job loss, marriage breakup – we could find out if we looked closer.] Something that the man in black's almost-bored tone implies he is disinclined to do. *[The physical and the mental never work independently; they are two sides of the same coin.]*

So why is he fixing the fence? The house doesn't even have a roof.

[Bigger repairs are beyond him. But to do nothing would be to give up completely. And even a broken mind must have some psychic boundaries.]

They watch him a moment: every time he tries to nail a board in place, the nail falls out, or he drops the hammer, or a wind arises from nowhere to blow it over, and he has to start all over again.

[Even if they're not very effective.]

Eventually, the man gives up on his desultory DIY, and trudges back towards the house. And as he does so there is a movement by the side of the shed, from which some shadow detaches and a vague, translucent form, subtly veined with strands of red and blue, moves silently after him with a dog-like lope.

What's that? Some part of him?

[*No. That's something else.*]

And they are back sat on the bench in the saturating fog.

But how did you do that? How did you get in?

[*There is no "getting in", you pea brain! That's what I was showing you: we're already "in". We just don't realise it.*]

So why don't *people realise it?* she asks, after an abashed silence. *That the mind isn't private?*

He looks at her, then back toward the busy square. [*Because we are schooled to build walls made of lies.*]

But I still don't understand how you get insi—I mean, how you . . . find that bigger place, whatever it is.

[*By going beyond self, by dismantling it.*] He shrugs. [*There are various techniques.*]

Such as what?

[*Enough theory for now, I think. Shall we try again?*]

And with that he stands up and walks off again into the crowd, out of which as he passes a face jumps out, and her eyes do a double-take.

For it is Fogler's.

HE IS SITTING ALONE at a square-side table at one of the café-bars, nursing a slim-necked bottle of something.

On sight of him, Squirrel ducks down, but he hasn't seen her. She circles round through the crowds, making her way to his blindside. What's he doing here?

Every now and then he lifts up his head and stares off into space, defocusing, his eyes twitching – checking his interface, with a fretful frequency. Is he waiting for something, someone?

She moves closer.

He takes another sip of his drink, and there is something about that deeply familiar movement – the slightly foppish turn of the wrist, the gnarled joint of the little finger daintily extended – that triggers something in her.

And just like that, with no preamble, she connects.

She is standing in the Den. It is dark – which it always is – but there is no one else around, which also means that it's late. She recognises by the knotted hands in front of her, the dirty bitten fingernails, that she is seeing through Fogler's eyes. He is bent over his little gaming tank, fiddling with something. A silhouette darkens the doorway, and he half-rises, his hand moving to the pocket of his ratty cardigan.

"Oh," he says. "It's you."

"Bit jumpy, aren't you?" says Denton.

"It's late, is all. Drink?"

The enforcer shakes his head.

"Need to have a word with you about something."

"In which case, maybe *I'll* have one," with a nervous half-laugh, "if you don't mind."

Denton waves a hand and Fogler moves to fix himself a glass of some fluorescent pink liquid, pored over chunks of ragged ice that he fetches from a bowl in the freezer, along with a shrivelled wedge of lime.

"Want an umbrella with that?" Denton scoffs.

[*Only if I can stab you in the eye with it,*] she hears him think.

"So what's it about," Fogler says, "this *word?*"

Denton lumbers over and begins to examine Fogler's gaming tank.

"Lily."

"Oh?"

Denton has picked up one of the gaming figures, and watches its little limbs bicycling fruitlessly, trying to position itself back into fighting stance.

"She's gotta go, Fogler, I'm afraid."

"Go where?" But from his strained tone, it's clear he already knows.

"She can't be trusted to do her job no more," Denton replies. "You know that. She's lost perspective."

Fogler sips his drink. Swallows.

"Don't worry, though," the enforcer continues. "I won't ask you to get your hands dirty." He chuckles, nodding down at Fogler's grubby fingers.

"Denton, I ..."

[*Say something. Do something, you coward.*]

"What?" Denton is staring at him, almost willing him for a pretext. But Fogler falls silent. Denton snorts, then turns to leave, in the process dropping the little combatant, which smacks onto the floor of the tank with a little thwack, and toils there on its back, trying and repeatedly failing to regain its feet.

"Anyway, just a head's up."

Fogler stares down into his glass.

And when he looks up again the view has switched, and she is stood there looking at the old man and his girly-pink drink and his sorry little gaming tank.

"Well, well, little Squirrel, and what are we doing still up?"

And a look of confusion comes over his face, then alarm, and all at once she is back in the square, watching his big bulbous head turn frantically this way and that, as he stands, scouring the people about him, and she ducks and burrows into the cover of the crowd.

YOU KNEW he would be there, Squirrel says in the boat on the way back to the mayor's house.

The man in black's mouth gives a little shrug. [*Given your response to my earlier mention of Denton, I figured that anyone from your time there might induce a similarly strong reaction. So I did a little research. Seems he drinks there quite often.*]

So what did they do with her?

[*With whom?*]

Lily!

[*You would have to ask them that,*] after too long a pause.

She looks away and down at her shadow in the passing water.

So that was how I was able to get in? she asks. *Because of how I feel about him?*

[*Deep familiarity is one way. Love, hate, fear, desire – almost doesn't matter. Anything that makes you forget yourself, that connects you with that other. Like houses, remember? We all share the same plumbing.*]

But if everyone has those connections, why can't they all read minds?

[*Because they're too wrapped up in their false selves to notice the possibility. They think the illusion they've been taught to believe in is real. But a Natural can see the truth, and take advantage of that. And once you know how, it's relatively easy. As I said, most people have no psychic defences at all.*]

And she'd done this without meeting Fogler's gaze. She's been talking with the man in black this whole time without seeing his eyes, nor he hers, but she'd assumed that was all his doing. What an idiot.

His laughter fills her head – a strange sensation, like having someone else's goosebumps.

So why the glasses, then? If the eyes don't matter?

[*That's just what I tell Friedler. Doesn't hurt to keep a few trade secrets. Besides,*] – he taps the frames with a finger – [*they do have certain other advantages.*]

Why didn't you tell me all this at the start?

He turns and grins.

[*What? And spoil all the fun?*]

CHAPTER FIVE

A JOURNEY BY WATER.

The boat rocks as she steps out; anxious hands, fearing the impropriety of touch, offer up support, but she needs none. The small party makes its way through the little stone archway and up the garden path as the waxing moon lays cool white accents on a ground of midnight blue.

She turns back, looking out from under the hooded cloak.

Mortlake never looked so lovely – much lovelier in fact than by day. It is a rambling place, with no unity of design, and no architectural features worth preserving. Years from now it will host the Royal Tapestry Works, and then a girl's school, until, much later still, all that remains will be a part of the garden wall and a little blue commemorative plaque (and of course, all that is gone now too). But things may look lovely by moonlight that would disappoint in the garish scrutiny of the sun.

The door opens before she reaches it, spilling warm candlelight along the stepping-stone path. The servant bows deep and wordlessly as she and one of her companions detach from the party and move through the doorway, where another servant is waiting to light them up the stairs to the library – for where else would he be?

They reach the door of his rooms, and she knocks gently. A frail voice mumbles back an inarticulate reply, but not actually frail, for it has always had that timbre, as if begrudging the effort of dragging his soaring spirit back to its prison of flesh.

She turns the door handle, and her companion moves to follow her, but she stops him.

"Your Grace, I—"

"Do not be foolish. I have known this man most my life."

And would trust him with it, Eva believes.

The room is sparsely lit, the peterings of a low fire grumble in the hearth, a branch of candles set upon a desk barely illuminates the man's face, much younger than he looks, and who is now sat, bent over a flat oval stone of obsidian black, slanted upright on a little stand, whispering to it fervently. What does he see in his black mirror? He ceases at her approach, covers the stone with a purple velvet cloth, and stands, lowering his head in a small bow.

"Please," she waves away the gesture, "let there be no distinctions between us this evening – except one: tonight I am but a humble scholar, and your pupil."

He smiles and chuckles at this, resigning himself to the conceit. "As you wish."

He motions to a stool the other side of the table at which he is standing, and she sits.

"And what would my pupil require of me this evening?" he asks.

Eva has given this a great deal of thought. Feeling at a bit of a loss, unsure what to do or whom to confide in, she has used up one of her only three help cards for this round in order to identify which of her inner circle of advisers can be most relied upon. And so here she stands before Doctor John Dee, Royal Astrologer and historically her most trusted confidant, whom the help card has confirmed is in fact an NPC and therefore *not* Azimuth himself, wondering whether the bookish scholar is too unworldly to help with her dilemma: should she marry? Yet in these times the decision is primarily a question of geopolitics – strategic alliances, the production of heirs and ensuring succession – not matters of the heart. But she cannot just come out and ask him directly – which would risk impropriety and likely offend or embarrass him. She therefore has to hint, and hope he plays along.

"It is question of pure mathematics," she says.

"Very well. It is a subject that lies within my compass," he adds modestly. "What is the issue?"

"Ah, that is it precisely: *issue* is the issue. For a lone figure to increase, it must have a multiplier, must it not?"

"Indeed it must, if it be *fruitful*."

He gets it! Thank God.

"And therein my dilemma lies – a most abstract and scholarly one, of course: by *which* quantity must it be multiplied?"

"By that which promises the greatest product. And yet," the doctor gets up and moves to rouse the guttering fire with a brass poker, "one must also be mindful of *quality*. For though some of shallow study would assert that numbers, being quantities, have a nature all alike, this is not so. Each has a character of its own, a quintessence, that speaks of its true meaning. *Per exemplorum gratia: One* is singular, determined, solitary; *two* is fertile, equanimous, companionable; *three* is restless, quarrelsome, ambitious. For myself, I have always had a fondness for *seven*, for it is the figure of completion, wholeness, totality; sufficient of itself and yet fecund with possibility. This we may best see geometrically. Following Euclid, we find that . . ."

And he's off – and not in a very helpful way. (She should have *seven* children? *Husbands?!*) Perhaps he doesn't get it after all, and needs *more* of a hint. She decides to reframe her metaphor.

"Good Doctor, I fear mathematics may be *too* abstract for our discourse. What then of heraldry?"

"It is also a subject in which I have some little proficiency."

"Which emblems best complement our English lions? The fleur-de-lys, the bear, the eagle, or the bull?"

Does she imagine it, or has a little light come on behind those famously watchful eyes?

"Pupil, if I may, these lions are leopards."

"How so?"

"They are *passant guardant,* and in this aspect – as the French heraldists insist – the English lion must properly be regarded a *léopard.* Now, as my pupil well knows, *leopardos* is the issue of *léon* and *pardos*, and like our common mule, he is himself without power of issue. Which, however, rather than symptom of his weakness, we take to be a sign of his strength, independence and purity. As we read in Prinsault, the *léopard* is also . . ." The voice growing less audible now as he moves distractedly off through the archway that leads to his study in search of some particular tome, out into the book-lined suite of rooms that are his obsession, and the envy of every scholar in Europe.

So she *shouldn't* marry? She might have the heart and stomach and of a king, but Elizabeth has the generative parts of a (not so) weak and feeble woman, and through her early reign she is not short of suitors eager to sow that fallow field with their own ripe seed (*ew*), and Eva's head is spinning with the potential geopolitical alliances. And yet, if she reads Dee's arcane hints correctly – leopards were, at the time, thought to be the infertile offspring of a male lion and a female panther – the answer lies not in the heraldic arms of the home-grown (and sadly already married) Earl of Leicester, nor her late sister Mary's Spanish leftovers, and not with French Dukes or Austrian Archdukes. Gloriana should go her own way, a proto-Eurosceptic, ploughing her own unseeded furrow, mistress with no master, a Virgin Queen chastely married to her people like a nun to Christ.

This, of course, is pretty much what the historical Elizabeth did – and quite a successful job she made of it, too. And yet, because she had no heir, within the curtailed course of a Jacobean lifespan the crown was to pass to a superstitious, vain and pleasure-loving oaf, and thence to his introverted and autocratic son, and the Golden Age was destined to fracture into civil war. But what – her goal in this particular round of *Sabotage* – can be done to prevent that? And so, naturally, Eva had thought that marriage was the way.

But then again, if Dee's advice can be trusted, maybe not.

But *is* it trustworthy? He is not Azimuth, as the help card has revealed, but has he been swayed into Azimuth's schemes? She thinks not. For there is something about him, her royal astrologer, that speaks to her. And not just his professed unswerving loyalty; his advice, she is sure – rambling, pedantic, convoluted and possibly mistaken as it may be – is sincere, well-meant. For he is his own man. And that is a rare and treasured quality – in any age.

ANOTHER MEETING, another place.

[*You wanted to see where we live.*]

And which would haunt his mind from that day forward, both waking and asleep.

Still not the silver city – which Caulden was beginning to fear he would never see – nor another environmental wasteland, but somewhere seeming more vibrant and alive. And indeed, it was at first glance very like a rainforest: a canopy of dark fronds overlapping above him, a thick carpeting of roots and vines interweaving underfoot. But closer inspection belied this initial impression, revealing leaves that were not leaves, roots and vines that were something else entirely, and the whole thing not organic at all – or at least,

not solely so. It was the colours, he decided. They were just
. . . well, *wrong*: arterial reds, electroluminescent blues, and
other jarring hues where vibrant yellows and salubrious
greens should be, all marbling through a substratum as
black as charred flesh.

All a bit bleak, to be frank. Lovecraft meets technofutur-
ism, perhaps.

[*You must not be afraid,*] the figure attempted to reassure
him. [*Your disquiet arises from the simple fact that you have
no reference point for this. But the aesthetic is secondary. Purpose dictates form, as it should. Try to put away your childish
associations.*]

Well, the associations of a child lost in some cybergothic
fairy-tale forest. And *what* purpose, exactly? Did he – *does* he
– want the answer to that question?

As in the other places they had shown him, he felt the
same ill-defined unease, the same vertiginous disconnect;
almost, he realised, a kind of awe – and was then hit by
what that word truly meant, how over time it had become
corrupted, diluted through frivolous misappropriation: *how
simply awful*; *wow, that's awesome*. But here was *truly* a thing
of awe, of dread. It was an *awful* place. Fitting, perhaps, for
creatures like gods – but *what* gods, he is still not sure.

They walked on, and the way had opened up into a broad
boulevard, still enclosed by the leafy canopy overhead, but
banked on either side by stepped terraces of the same funereal
techno-jungle. It was strange to walk on it; each footstep felt a
trespass, an imposition – almost something for which he
should apologise or ask permission. But to whom, or what?

[*Your reaction is normal.*]

Not very reassuring. And how could it say that? How could it know what it was customary for someone like him – from his culture and time – to feel? And then he understood.

"I am not the first here, am I?"

[*There have been others.*]

Had there been a hesitation, there, a reluctance?

"When?" He turned to look at the creature, whose features, by virtue alone of their alien unfamiliarity, were always inscrutable, but at that moment were even more unreadable, mask-like, as if there were another face – many faces – hidden from him for his own benefit, shifting about beneath.

[*That is not a question that makes sense in the way that you think it does.*]

"How many, then?"

[*A few.*]

The boulevard came to an end and began to slope down into an enormous bowl-shaped space, like an auditorium or amphitheatre, looming at the centre of which was a colossal statue. It depicted a gargantuan humanoid figure – female, in fact – perched on a seat or throne raised upon a dais. It was reminiscent in some respects of the statues of Rameses at Luxor, or the giant Buddhas of China, but beyond that he had no basis for comparison, for it was far greater in size, dwarfing anything that Earth's history had to offer; and greater in fact than any he had so far seen here, which together with the jungle vibe reminded him of the temples of Cambodia, of Angkor Wat, the crumbling ruins co-opted by – even *inter-breeding* with – the forests that slowly consumed them.

But like their other statues, it too was moving, breathing in and out, swaying, twitching. And as their slow procession neared, its gaze shifted, and it stared down; it watched them.

His bowels began to melt, his breathing to shift into a shallow pant. He wanted to be sick, to shit, to run, to curl up into a ball and cry.

[*Do not be afraid,*] his guide repeated. [*Your response is not uncommon, even among our own people. You may think of it as just a statue, a representation. As something symbolic.*]

But when were their statues ever "just" statues? However, gradually, despite himself, a calm had begun to descend upon him, his nausea to dissipate, his anxiety to lessen. Had the creature done that, somehow?

The slope was stepped with more terraces, which he and the creature descended in lateral curves, moving down more directly here and there via short ramps. It was, Caulden realised, a sort of labyrinth.

And with his head and stomach more settled, he could give the looming giantess his less bilious scrutiny.

The statue was indeed female; in fact, strikingly beautiful, albeit in a somewhat severe way: like his guide, it possessed the same large, dark eyes, the same hint of a nose, but also a stronger, squarer jaw, more prominent cheekbones; and the upper body, about which its overlong arms and hands swept in softly graceful arcs, was full and womanly, the breasts exposed, painted or tattooed with labyrinthine markings of their own.

But this was where all human resemblance ended.

Some aspects diverged not in type but in quantity: the arms doubling on both sides, a third eye set centrally in her forehead, and with almost cartoonish nightmare, one also atop each breast where the nipple should be – of which, as the figure shifted, he saw that there were actually three. Other features were, he supposed, borrowed from their plant or animal kingdoms, but acquired in places an almost architectural symmetry of design: above her face, her forehead – though, like his guide, whether hair, bone or headdress was impossible to say – rose into a stepped structure like a ziggurat, beside and on top of which, horn- and antennae-like, sprouted a plethora of curling and twitching things. But it was the lower body that was the most grotesque, the full swollen abdomen of a spider or a bee, and either side of which bestrode a set of scorpion-like legs, ending in pincered points.

God alone knew where his mind had dredged the literary recollection (as with all his visits, Azimuth not being available to prompt him), but he found himself reminded of *Lear*:

> But to the girdle do the gods inherit,
> Beneath is all the fiends'.

And throughout it all, the same red and blue marbling – even into the irises of her enormous eyes, barely visible at the fringes of those huge dilated pupils – and he had noticed then something that should have been evident from the first, but his mind had been too boggled to process: she was not *sat* on her throne, but *part* of it. And it, too, was one with the whole of the surrounding landscape, all the vines that were not vines, tendrils that were not tendrils, each not-leaf and not-branch, channelling whatever energy or power they conveyed toward the centre and the regal figure that was their flowering – or, perhaps, their source?

It was like some crazy art installation, or some deeply disturbing VR game – which some diminishingly small part of him still prays to be the case.

[*You are right,*] said the creature, answering his previous unvoiced observation. [*She is all one, and we are all She.*]

It went on to explain how the whole place was both temple and mausoleum, hatchery and burial ground. How around them lay both those who had lived and those who had yet to be born – but really, there was no such distinction to be made, for all lived on in Her body, in Her presence.

[*Would you like to meet Her?*] it asked.

EVA DECIDES to take a break from her royal duties.

After succumbing successively to a Spanish Armada (cannily bolstered by French mercenaries), her deposition at the hands of Mary Queen of Scots (that perfidious Norfolk!), and no less than three assassinations by ladies-in-waiting, she decides to try another tack. The Queen, it transpires, is not always the most powerful piece on the board.

She will become an actor!

But since there are no females allowed on the Elizabethan stage, this means her piece must be male (now *there's* a

Shakespearean pun . . .). She settles upon a young aspiring thesp, whom she christens Orlando Woolf (she can't resist the anachronistic literary nod), and sees to it that he becomes apprenticed to the Lord Chamberlain's Men – the Bard's own company! This does mean that her access to the royal court is curtailed, somewhat, but not cut off entirely, for though the Queen will not stoop so low as to attend the Globe, she is quite happy for the Globe to come to her. And so eventually, having worked his way up through the roles of stagehand, dresser, gopher, *Johannes Factotum* and . . . well, let's just say that her little Jack really *has* turned his hand to all trades . . . her young player will eventually catch the regal eye through his (her?) delightfully whimsical Titania and defiantly spirited Beatrice at successive royal command performances.

But all the shifting identities – normally a delight, and her favourite part of *Sabotage*: to inhabit another's skin, another's mind – are beginning to take their toll. Something about the nature of acting, perhaps, of the layered deceits and pretences of Elizabethan theatre? Until, during one drizzly matinée performance of *Twelfth Night*, she realises that she is a woman, playing a man, who is playing a woman, who has *disguised* herself as a man, but is in love with a man who doesn't know that "she" is a woman, fending off the unwanted romantic attentions of a woman who thinks she is a man, and she feels her mind teetering on the brink of some vertiginous psychological precipice, her blank verse dying in her throat as she begins to wonder if *any* of this is real, or whether it is simulations all the way down (or up?).

And so it is almost with relief that a wandering cannonball, earlier rolled across the painted "heavens" to simulate thunder during the storm scene, drops "inadvertently" through the "poorly secured" hatchway above (thank you, Azimuth) and brains her (his? her?) poor Viola, mid soliloquy.

And she finds that the game is starting to pall, and that the part she wants to play most of all – if only she knew what that were – is herself.

THE CREATURE IGNORES her presence, licking patiently at its wounds.

Though, strictly speaking, the Globe and the other theatres are in fierce competition with the bull- and bear-baiting pits, the opportunity for financial gain ignores all such partisan loyalties, and so her young Orlando's portfolio of duties has lately extended to include part-time zookeeper, maintaining an eye on the weekly dwindling menagerie that is now the joint concern of Messrs Burbage, Burbage, Hemminges, Phillips, *et alia*. But actually, it is mostly the dogs that are dwindling, the baits presenting a fairly one-sided match, and the loss of a bear is mourned almost as moderns would bemoan the death of a celebrity. Blind Bess, this one is known as, curiously. Perhaps that's why it's ignoring her; although, she notes, it "sees" well enough to tend to itself, as it sits there grooming, licking its paws and rubbing them over its ears and face like a cat.

Still, it is astonishing to Eva that such barbarity can exist a mere stone's throw from some of the most sublime human sentiment ever to tread the boards or grace a page. And yet, everything about this age was a paradox, during which humans were treated little better than animals – especially if you had the misfortune to get on the wrong side of Francis Walsingham's secret police. Now *he* would have been an ideal piece – an extensive spy network already at his disposal, the trust and ear of the Queen – but an NPC, unfortunately. And would she have had the stomach for it? Walsingham's "methods" were not for the faint of heart. Could she torture, maim, terrorise, all in the name of the greater good? Even in a game such as this? She's not sure she could. The threat of burning at the stake, of hanging, drawing and quartering, lopping off ears, needles under the fingernails, stocks and pillories, racks and pits, the Little Ease and the Scavenger's Daughter – and a surprising amount of it for participative public entertainment. It was an age when cruelty, disease and death were commonplace, mundane occurrences, each day a chimera of the angelic and the bestial.

And yet, have *we* changed that much? She hears stories, even now, snippets of rumours that she is not supposed to . . . of *bouts*, of places out in the wilds where . . . well, she doesn't know what, exactly, but her imagination has had a go. And if things like that *still* happen, despite all our sup-posed "progress" – technological, moral and aesthetic – then what does that say about humanity? What's that quote? Something about a crooked timber, or a tree that can never grow straight? (For the sake of fairness, while the game is in progress, Azimuth is not here to ask, and so without him her monitored access to the Feeds is blocked. But something like that, she thinks.)

Or just the one about an old dog and new tricks, maybe. Is that all morality is, then? A trick? A sham?

She looks again at the bear's sad face – is it really sad, or is that just her own anthropomorphic projection? An external representation of her own predicament, perhaps, "chained" to this place, this game? But how could it *not* feel pain? How would any sentient creature feel, manacled to a stake, baited and "worried" by packs of snarling mastiffs? But she feels sorry for the dogs too, and has no doubt that all the furry combatants involved feel fear and suffering – they must do; all they lack is a voice with which to tell us.

And ironically, just at that very thought, the bear turns to her with surprisingly soulful blind eyes.

"Eva?" it says. "Is that you?"

CHAPTER SIX

PERCY'S ARMS FLAIL in panic, adrenaline flooding his body as he struggles to get up, and again immediately regrets it as a stab of pain scythes through his chest, his arms crumpling with weakness. He slumps back defeated. In contrast, Cherri – Abi – merely nods to the new arrival in casual greeting.

"Inspector," she says, "I believe you've already met Camillo."

The man in black gives a jaunty little finger wave.

"You *know* him?"

"If it wasn't for Camillo, you'd be fish food."

"Well, *technically*," corrects the man in black, "I did also *set* those fish on you. Call it quits?" His mouth erupts in a delighted grin, while his eyes remain inscrutable behind the black visor.

"I . . . I don't understand."

"It was Camillo told me what had happened," says Abi, "where you'd be."

And now Percy connects where he'd previously seen Abi's black "wetsuit", a twin to the one now sported by the man in black.

"And how do you know *him*?" He nods at the man she calls Camillo.

"Another long story, I'm afraid," she says. "Which can wait until tomorrow. Come on," rearranging his blankets, "you need your rest."

"But you *work* for Friedler," Percy says to the man. "How can you—the heads! On the wall!"

"I do acknowledge some occasional conflicts of interest," Camillo replies mock-contritely, his mouth now dropping in a comically exaggerated pout.

"But how can you—"

"Rest!" Abi chides once more, as if to an over-tired child. She nods again at Camillo, who disappears down the hallway. "Look, you're safe here, I promise," laying her hand on his. "We'll speak more tomorrow."

"Safe? I—"

"Tomorrow," she repeats.

She leans over, switches off the lamp.

Is he safe? If not, he's in no shape to make a run for it. And why would they rescue him if they bore him subsequent ill will? But the pain and lethargy eventually addle this internal debate, and he is powerless to do other than meekly watch Abi head off in the same direction as the man in black.

THE NEXT THING HE KNOWS it is morning, and he is waking to emaciated light seeping through the cracked, moss-fringed windows.

There is no sign of Abi or Camillo. He rubs his chest, which still feels tender, but a little better, and tentatively he sits up. The thing on his wrist has gone, leaving only a slight bruising and a dot of red on the back of his hand where it had plugged into his vein. He desperately needs to pee, presumably in consequence of the amount of the lagoon he's swallowed, rather than Abi's soup.

He makes to stand, succeeding at the third attempt, and shuffles off along the same corridor down which Abi had followed the man in black, hoping his explorations turn up a toilet, or something that will serve as one, feeling ridiculous and vulnerable in what he recognises now as a woman's nightie.

The place is ramshackle, but a concerted effort has gone into clearing, cleaning and repurposing certain areas within it – an impromptu kitchen, some sleeping quarters, and hopefully somewhere a place to empty his bladder. He turns a corner and makes down another corridor lined with damp-mottled information boards on local history, coal mines, slate quarries and copper works, and spies at its end a little featureless graphic of a figure of a man that promises facilities for relief. He is making his way toward this when he passes another door, slightly ajar, the dark within pierced enticingly with little blue, red and green pinpricks of flickering light. He edges quietly toward it, and pushes it open.

Amid a tangle of cables, screens, and boxes big and small, is a reclining chair, like a dentist's, and in which now reclines Abi, only her red mouth visible, clad head to food in her black wetsuit-type-thing, her eyes hidden behind those large reflective goggles, and bundles of fibres emerging from various parts of her. Some sort of full-immersion VR thing?

On the wall behind this setup there is a large screen, on which is playing out a curious scene. It is a theatre of some sort, but one from long ago, judging by the swashbuckling shirts, breeches and tights, the bumrolls, ruffs, hooped skirts and corsets. A rowdy crowd is heckling and laughing, eating, chatting, throwing food, while the actors – on a raised wooden platform, mere inches from the boisterous audience – plough on undeterred, as if such football-crowd behaviour were par for the theatrical course.

There is a little clearing of the throat behind him, and he turns.

"Nice outfit," says the man in black.

"SO WHAT IS ALL THIS?" Percy asks, gesturing at the roomful of equipment. "Some sort of VR gig?"

Camillo pulls a face. "Yes and no," he says, and turns back toward Abi, who is sat up now, as he helps her to detach various cables from various body parts.

"And this?" Percy points at the screen.

"It's a game," Abi says, pulling off her gloves. "But we think it's also more than that."

"Like what?"

"Some way to control them, to *retrain* them, somehow. Eva, I mean – and the other Naturals."

"You think she's still alive?"

She shrugs and looks away, busying herself with detaching other straps and wires.

He looks again at the screen.

"That's . . . is that Shakespeare's Globe?"

"I'm impressed, Antonio. Didn't pin you as a drama buff."

"Well, it is quite iconic. So the game is based around that?"

"That's one of the time periods. There've been other scenarios: the French Revolution, the Russian Revolution, the Roman Empire in the time of Pompey and Caesar – they seem to like their revolutions and civil strife."

"And you think this is connected to Friedler?"

"And Caulden. Maybe other Arcs too."

"The Arcs? I don't think that very likely. I mean—"

The man in black stops what he's doing and stands up, looking Percy in the face, though his gaze is still hidden behind his trademark lenses.

"Your employers are scum, I'm afraid, Inspector. All is not what it seems with the arcologies."

"I'd had a spider crawling the Arc's systems for some time," Abi says, "looking for any trace of her. Which is what first drew me here – and how I eventually met Camillo. He was looking for someone, too. The spider flagged that something weird was going on with the Arc's main AI."

"Weird how?"

"Running some very processing-intensive simulations. Could be something, could be nothing, so we decided to infiltrate it to find out. Turns out to be this game, called *Sabotage*." She motions at the screen. "High-fidelity, total immersion VR. We think it's basically a behavioural modification environment. Uses scenarios to gameplay learning, to suggest and embed behavioural changes. It's very clever."

"But even if the Arc is running this . . . this *Sabotage* game," Percy says, "why did you think that was a sign that someone there had abducted Eva? And even if they have her, why would this game lead you to her? I mean, it could be anything. Arcologies provide all sorts of bespoke entertainments for residents. It could be an educational thing, some project to engage history buffs or war games enthusiasts."

But Abi is already shaking her head. "Too resource-intensive for that. It uses up a *lot* of computational juice. I mean, you don't deploy those kind of resources just for the kicks of some geopolitical cosplayers."

"Even so, I—"

"It's because she's a Natural," Camillo butts in. "A very powerful one. They have been collecting them for a while, now."

"Collecting?"

"Which is why Caulden needs Friedler. For his cloning skills, too."

"But this is crazy. I mean, do they really *believe* in this superstitious—"

"See?" Camillo turns to Abi. "Wasting our time." His black lenses stare right through Percy. "Maybe I should have left you for the fishes. Or maybe you want a demonstration? Maybe I—"

"Camillo." Abi glares down the black-lensed eyes, which reflect her stare for a moment, and he waves a dismissive hand and walks off out of the room.

"Sorry," Abi says. "He's . . . it's been hard on him, working for Friedler. I keep worrying he might snap. We've tried to save who we can, but we have to weigh that up against the chance of bringing the whole thing down."

She begins to pack up a coil of wires, dismantling the setup, taking up where Camillo left off.

"Cash your chips or risk it all for the jackpot – I understand," Percy concedes. "It's a common dilemma in law enforcement. But even if they are engaged in illegal activities – abduction, cloning, whatever – I still don't get why. What would motivate that?"

"Because, as Camillo said, they were all Naturals. All the missing people. That's the one common denominator."

"But even if someone *believed* in that," he says as she eyes him coolly, "what would they use them *for*?"

She shrugs. "Camillo has theories."

Percy sighs and looks up at the screen. "So what's your plan? With the game."

"It's tricky to get in. We can manage it briefly, for stretches at a time, but the AI is top-notch, and so is its security."

"And have you managed to contact her?"

"A couple of times."

"And what happened?"

"She didn't recognise me." She has replaced the same red-stoned ring after taking off the gloves, and is now twisting it around her finger – a characteristic gesture, he's coming to realise. "The game is incredibly immersive, so there are times while you're playing where it's like a dream almost, where you aren't even *aware* that there is an outside. So we're trying to find ways of creating anomalies that may jar her out of it. As I say, it's worked a couple of times, but . . . well, the last attempt didn't end so well."

"The fall," making the connection. "That was your rescue attempt."

"She was supposed to wait for our signal. Maybe she slipped. Or maybe . . ."

She looks down again.

"Like lucid dreaming," Percy says.

"Sorry?"

"Looking for anomalies? I used to be interested in that."

"Did you, now?" She grins. "Were you any good at it?"

"Afraid not. Seems I like my sleep too much. These days, I can't even remember having dreamt at all. Maybe I don't, anymore."

"I don't think we ever stop dreaming." Abi stands up from the box of wires. "So will you help us? I mean, seems like you could do with some friends."

That, at least, is something of which Percy doesn't feel in need of further proof.

ABI DIRECTS HIM to his freshly dried clothes and shoes, still warm from the heater, and Percy returns to the VR room to find her taping up the last of the boxes, having finished putting away the setup.

"Are you leaving?" he asks, nodding at the boxes. "Because of me?"

"It's OK," she says. "We've got another place. But yeah, figure they'll start exploring the lagoon now, once they work out you didn't turn into mermaid chow." She puts down the packing tape and looks at him. "Why don't you come with us?"

"I think I should head back to the hotel," he says.

"Well *that's* stupid. There's no way it'll be safe there, now."

"I can't hide. I have a job to do."

"Look, this good sheriff schtick is very noble, and all that, but this is not some playground bullying you're standing up to. It'll get you killed. Again."

"I will still help you, in whatever way I can. I mean, we have the same objectives, more or less."

"What good's your help if you're dead?"

"Perhaps you underestimate me."

"Like I underestimated your scuba diving skills?" She smiles. "Well, if you're determined to offer your head up for target practice, perhaps you can be of some use. We need to get someone inside the Arc. I mean, actually *physically* inside."

"You're still convinced she's in there somewhere?"

"Whatever's left of her is still my sister."

A philosophically dubious assertion, but he notices her playing with the ring again, and resists telling her so.

"And you trust Camillo?" he asks her.

"Why would I not? He's lost people, too."

"How do you know he's not using you in some way?"

"For what?"

"I don't know. To find more people like your sister?"

"Look, Antonio, I'm a gut person, and my gut says I can trust him. Just like it knew I could trust you."

"That's really no way to establish relationships."

"Well, it's never served me wrong."

She grabs a box and sets it down on top of another.

"So what do you want me to do?" he asks.

"Have you met with the Director yet?"

He guesses she already knows that he has, but nods anyway.

"Can you arrange another meeting? A face-to face, to update him, or something?"

"I suppose so. For what purpose?"

"So you can let us in the back door."

ABI'S BOAT DROPS Percy on the mainland, a quiet little back-street canal.

"Be safe," she says as she restarts the engine.

"You've been watching me the whole time, haven't you?"

"We needed to find out how straight an arrow you were," beginning to pull the boat away.

"And?"

"Rigid as they come," she shouts back, and disappears off in her little black stealth skiff.

He walks the rest of the way to the hotel.

The fog is finally lifting, but only to be replaced by an unseasonable mugginess, which now permeates the afternoon air and seeps into his clothes, as if they never truly dried from his watery misadventures of the night before – or was it the night before that?

The Empire Hotel is unchanged by the weather, impervious to its charms or depredations, and looks equally dilapidated in the sunshine.

His reappearance at reception produces the most extreme reaction yet, as the young woman behind the counter stops whatever she's doing and just stares at him, slack jawed. Well, now he nows what it takes to pierce that facade of distracted boredom: coming back from the dead. Which would also confirm his suspicion that the staff here are Friedler's eyes and ears.

His room, predictably, has been thoroughly ransacked. Clothes strew the floor and the bed, his bag and case dismembered, their linings torn, as if mauled by some massive beast with a particular penchant for luggage. The data block from the Arc has gone, and of course the girl's implant, as has his personal tablet, and even for some reason his electric toothbrush. Something peeks out from under the bed. He bends down and retrieves his stun baton – the only weapon he owns, and not much of one, considering the Goliath he must face.

He sits down on the bed, amid the mess.

And yet, all David needed was his slingshot.

"Call Director Caulden," he instructs his virtual assistant.

He gets the Director's equivalent – some digital composite of vocal intonation and facial characteristics calculated to charm or disarm, as required.

"The Director sends his sincerest apologies, Inspector, but he's afraid that he is very busy at the moment. Can I take a message?"

OK, if he wants to play it like that. Percy's had enough of all this pussy-footing around – a term that, if his straight-spoken Yorkshire grandmother could be relied on, didn't come from the delicately feline little sidesteps people took to avoid saying what they really meant, but from something more crudely direct: "Stop your piss-farting around and come out with it." Which, ironically, makes "pussy-footing" itself a form of pussy-footing, a mealy-mouthed aversion to calling a spade a spade – or a turd a turd.

Well, the time has come to shit or get off the pot.

"Yes, that's fine," he tells the virtual assistant. "I have just the one message: Could you please ask the Director when he might be available for a game of *Sabotage*?"

CHAPTER SEVEN

[*IT'S A FAILURE of imagination,*] he tells her, from wherever he is.

Maybe if I had an actual human to practice on, Squirrel grumbles.

[*A poor tradeswoman blames her tools.*]

The last few weeks have been spent mostly stuck in her room, trying to hone her invasion skills, with mixed results.

But it's hard. There is a knack to it, evidently, one which cannot be consciously mastered, but must employ a combination of instinct and intuition. The fact that she has already achieved this multiple times, albeit unpredictably, just makes it all the more frustrating.

But it doesn't even have any thoughts!

[*How do you know that? Besides, thoughts aren't just verbal or conceptual. They are intuitions, desires, images, memories, feelings. You just have to open yourself.*]

She tries again. But the little hamster refuses to give up its secrets, merely picks up another one of the sunflower seeds that Squirrel has strewn around its little cage and happily stuffs it in its already fat cheek for later. Which is ironic, really – her continued failure – as they both know what it's like to be a captive guinea pig.

[*OK, let's try again tomorrow. The Old Man wants to see you now.*]

What old man? And with a cardiac lurch she realises that this is his nickname for Friedler himself.

The chaperdrone leads her back through the servants' corridors, down the way she'd gone when she'd first left her hospital cell. The man in black is waiting for her in the corridor that leads to the menagerie.

Why am I coming back here?

[*You're not,*] he thinks, and gestures to the wooden door at the other end – the one she's never been through. [*Be good,*] he warns her.

The room is filled with wood – walls of wood panelling, shelves, furniture. More than she's ever seen in one place. He sees her looking.

[*I know, right?*] He laughs. [*It's like he thinks it grows on trees.*]

But more than the wood, what catches her eye are the rows and rows of mounted heads.

Are those for real? she asks.

[*Pray that's a question you never get the answer to.*]

They are mostly non-human – or not wholly so. Perhaps that's where the failed experiments go – like Squirrel herself, if all this doesn't go well?

There is a leather armchair next to a fireplace with a small table next to it, but no one is sat there. Evidently, they must wait. The man in black wanders over to the hearth, takes up a poker from a stand and begins to coax the slumbering coals back to life. She watches the flames play in the reflections on his visor.

So what are the glasses actually for? she asks.

[*Maybe if you're a good little tree rodent, and you work really really hard, one day you'll get a pair of your own.*]

There is a noise at the far end of the room, and in through another door comes Friedler; the same – or similar – well-tailored outfit that she remembers from the eyrie, the same waistline fighting to be kept in check.

"Ah, our guest." He scans her from head to foot and back again, avoiding direct contact with her eyes. "And how are we today? Fully mended, I hope?"

[*Play nice.*]

She nods.

"Good, good." He takes a seat while they remain standing by the fireplace. "Camillo tells me you've been making good progress."

Squirrel's eyes flick involuntarily to the man in black.

[*Damn.*] He smirks. [*My secret identity is blown.*]

She looks back at Friedler and nods again.

"So, are we ready for a test run?"

"Perhaps not quite yet," Camillo says.

"Oh, I think she's bored, stuck in here every day, like a caged animal. But you're not, are you, little Squirrel?" His eyes rove up and down her once more. "Not anymore."

She shrugs.

"Let's see what you can do, shall we?"

THIS IS WHERE all the servants have gone.

They've been replaced. The odd bit of rent-a-muscle, the occasional Camillo with his special set of skills, maybe a chef or two, but otherwise the rest of the Mayor's household had been ripe for upgrade to the steel and polycarbonate simulacra that now weave and float between the guests, furnishing drinks and snacks with – in comparison to their human predecessors – an almost preternatural skill and grace.

[*Aren't you enjoying yourself?*]

Squirrel scans the roof terrace and spies Camillo across the other side, observing proceedings from a quiet corner within warming distance of the firepit.

That's not exactly how I'd describe it, she tells him.

[*Again with the ingratitude. We should have left you for the crabs to pick at.*]

But there is indeed little for her to enjoy. She's forbidden to eat or drink, and her only job is to stand by, looking ambiguously official in her new black uniform (minus stealth capacities, unfortunately), tasked with garnering surreptitious informational tidbits from Friedler's guests' mentally unguarded moments. She is sweeping, just as she's always done, only with a different set of tools.

The attendees are not dissimilar in look from the people she had seen in the eyrie at the Bouts: the young and the beautiful; or else those whom age has robbed of these qualities – or nature never gifted them – but which have been expensively and artificially re-bestowed; and, in some cases, qualities beyond even those. The tail-twins are here, slipping between the small groups with the lissom grace of calf-rubbing cats; someone else sporting a leopardskin mottling all down her long naked back; another with a cute little set of horns and a pair of elfin-tipped ears. But the tone is understated, tasteful, avoiding the cruder, more outlandish mods she'd see daily in the neighbourhood around the Den. What is commonly affordable becomes common, and therefore useless as a means of distinction from those who can afford much more.

And of course, that same money will also buy them technological advantages, far beyond the standard – fantastic processing speed, enormous storage capacity, and top-notch security protocols (which, with her own implant still out of commission, she won't tonight have opportunity to test).

As a reward for her recent good behaviour, she and her chaperdrone have graduated from her little sub-aquatic bedsit into a slightly larger room in the upper house, which even comes with its own above-ground window overlooking the orchards in the back gardens (so *that's* where the bananas come from). But this is the first time she's been up to the roof terrace – the first time, in fact, she's ever had such a view of the city, looking out through a rare clear night, the twinkling of lights bobbing in the lagoon, the hustle of Market Square and Founders Way, the muffled hubbub of others' lives, others' desires, cares and struggles, wafting up on the breeze like an exotic scent to be savoured. It's amazing what distance can do, the illusion of peacefulness it provides; like a war seen from space. Even the docks look quaint.

"Toilets?"

She stares back blankly at the face that has materialised before her.

"Hello? Anyone at home?"

It is the mark; from the bookstall.

Isn't it?

She points dumbly towards the glass-walled structure at the centre of the terrace, at which the face sighs melodramatically and moves off.

Yes. Yes, it *is* him; his manner is different, but that face – the one that had looked down on her with such genuine concern, as the strange vision that swam before her inner eye had faded – *that* face she won't forget.

Her eyes follow him, wait until he re-emerges from the facilities, and begin to stalk him at a distance. He rejoins his party, a small group of three, making a loud, crude observation about the resemblance between what he's recently flushed away and the tray of hors d'oeuvres proffered by a passing drone, at which his companions laugh.

It's almost like it's a different man – not the kindly, bookish gent that had even offered to arrange medical help at his own expense. *Could* he be?

She sidles closer, moving behind the cover of a large-leafed plant in a free-standing pot, its enormous flower opening up like the throat of some outlandish musical instrument, and begins to tune in. Like trying to pick out a single note from a song playing in a bar, trying to filter out everything that is *not* his thoughts – not just the chatter and the clink of glasses, the murmur of the fountain, the crackle of the fire and the distant sounds of the city, but also the psychic hubbub of his neighbours' mental jabber.

[*Don't force things,*] Camillo has told her. [*Let it come of its own accord.*]

And then she has it.

She's in.

He is in an apartment of some kind. There is music – soothing, instrumental, no strident motifs or catchy riffs, but audio balm, for atmosphere only – though she senses from the man's mood that it's not having its desired effect. She watches through his eyes as he sips from a cut-glass tumbler, hears the clink of ice, feels the cold burn of the alcohol. A little graphic of a speaker appears, top-right, and a minus sign flashes next to it, twice, as he turns down the music. He is uneasy.

This must be inside the Arc – that much she had guessed about bookstall man's origins, even before she'd tried to hack him; and the view from his window confirms it. She soaks up all the detail she can – the stylishly comfortable sofa and chairs, the pristine wall-screen and VR suite, the chattily attentive appliances, chirruping with solicitous babble as he passes. It's all very compact, very neat, but these same qualities also imbue the space with a smothering, claustrophobic air; an all-mod-cons cell optimised for sole occupation.

A menu overlay suddenly interrupts the view; he flicks desultorily through the Feeds – a documentary on the Haze problem in the underwater prisons, updates on the Secession

War in the States, an interactive car chase from an action film trailer, a VR period drama – all hold his attention for a micro-second before he moves on. Nothing is doing it for him today. He is restless, almost as if, despite all the creature comforts and opportunities for pleasant distraction, he is missing something more basic and vital, something intrinsic to who he is.

But what?

She suggests he looks about the apartment – she is getting a feel for that now, for how to redirect the PoV. She had assumed that memories are fixed, unalterable experiences, but Camillo has shown her that they are in fact *recreated anew* with each recall. And so, if done subtly, the little changes and tweaks she makes can be secreted among the mark's own little subconscious self-adjustments.

He gets up, stretches, and wanders over to the window, pokes in the kitchen cupboards, stares into the fridge, watches the bots change the sheets on his bed, clean his bathroom. But there used to be something else, didn't there? Something he liked to do? What was it?

She nudges him, a mental whisper.

Books.

And there is a flinch, a physical twinge, and he moves his hand up to his head as if to stifle a stab of pain.

She has to be careful now, or she will wake him from his reverie.

She prompts again, but more gently – just an image of the market, at the periphery of his vision, a stall with rows of cracked-spined paperbacks.

He half turns, facing a corner of the room that another part of him does not want—does not *allow* himself to look in. Where *is* he looking?

[*Remember,*] Camillo has said, [*a mental space is never merely a literal one.*]

She hadn't known what that had meant, and he'd had to explain it, but what happens next is a textbook illustration. There has appeared on his shelf – not there until now – a paperback book, a mental twin of one he might once have owned: itself a curious thing, some sci-fi or fantasy novel, heavily thumbed, its pages furred, its creased cover depicting a bizarre scene, a fluorescent tree hosting a plethora of strange animals, each one a surreal twist on some half-recognisable species – like Friedler's menagerie. It's fascinating to see what forms her suggestions take – but no time for her to examine it now. At her further prompting, he picks it up, opens it, flicks through the pages, and in doing so – as in a dream – the words becoming illegible, starting to swim and shift, to drift apart – he is now moving toward them, between them, into a space that is beyond words, beyond the room; into some other place, some other part of himself.

They are in a corridor, heading for a lift. He has a growing feeling that he shouldn't be here, shouldn't be remembering this – *is* it a memory? *His* memory? She tries to distract him from this path of analysis, luring his focus back into the details: the spartan finishing of the lift's interior, not even any buttons or display panels. Simply a utilitarian brushed steel box. He enters, and it begins to descend. Why is he going *there*? *Should* he be going there? Where *is* there?

She feels the pull of the decent on her (his) legs, the gravity-lag catching up with her as it finally stops. And the doors open.

A dream-like jump, and he now finds himself on some sort of balcony or platform – though not "he", for he shouldn't be here, shouldn't . . . should he? But where is . . . She brings him back again to the view, suggests that he shifts his head, alters his viewpoint – and there it is: an enormous enclosed space, the low, periodically spaced lighting somehow appropriate to this underground, this – what is it? What is he doing here? He doesn't know – *cannot* know. For it is a secret. But once he *did* know – didn't he? And lined up before him, the rows of cases, like glass coffins – row upon row upon row – and all the people inside them.

Who are they? she asks.

"I'm not supposed . . ." he mutters to himself, "no one is supposed . . ."

Go closer, she says.

And despite himself, at her suggestion he is down now among them – down where he shouldn't be, knee-deep in things he shouldn't remember.

There are little lights on the side of each case. He taps the glass of one, and an array of figures and glyphs brighten up the air before him. Shouldn't really have done that – he's just curious, now it's all finished, what he's been working on all this time. Who are they all?

He walks on, past other fogged up faces. All colours, all sizes and ages. The faces of women, of girls, of boys, of men—

She/he stops.

—of Lily.

She is outside him now, no longer a PoV, the shock of Lily's face breaking the meld of his mind with hers, throwing her out again into the party, and she is turning back to the man, questioning with her eyes, searching his face for answers.

"Thief," he says, almost to himself. And then louder. "Thief." Until he is shouting. Thief! Thief!"

Past him, over his shoulder, she sees Camillo.

[*Dear sweet girl,*] he says. [*I knew you would be trouble.*]

"AH, SO THAT WAS YOU, at the bookstall!" says Friedler. "What an interesting little coincidence."

They are gathered – Squirrel, Friedler, Camillo, two well-upholstered thugs, and her ever-present chaperdrone – back in the wood-furnished room. Friedler is sat in his chair before the fire, sipping his whiskey, while the rest of his entourage stand about him.

"We had little hints that he'd been compromised in some non-technical way," he continues. "The man himself remained oblivious, but I thought we'd better wipe him anyway; you know, as a precaution."

"Wipe?" she asks.

"His memories, his personality. Always better to recycle than to discard, and all that, times being what they are." He chuckles. "We could still use his intelligence, his skills.

Seems we didn't wipe thoroughly enough. Anyway, we have other uses for him."

So this is what Squirrel had seen: they had partitioned him like a hard drive, kept his work on this project – whatever it is – secret even from himself, and when she'd compromised him, they'd wiped him, formatted him, and installed a new personality, a new self, ready to be encoded with whatever purposes Friedler had in mind. But memory is a stubborn thing, and the fragments had persisted, were still *there* somewhere, still readable at a layer of being beyond digitisation – to such as Squirrel, anyway.

"Is that what you did to Lily?"

"I'm sorry?"

"The finder," prompts Camillo, who stands at the fireplace, agitatedly coaxing it back to life with the same ornate brass-handled poker.

"Ah, the hooker, you mean?" Friedler says. "So she was your friend, was she? Well, well. Small world indeed. She was a Natural too – did you know that? One of our best finders. Takes one to know one, I suppose. Didn't turn you in, evidently. We knew she'd lost a taste for the work; so sadly, we lost a use for her. Well, now she has a different use too."

"What do you mean? Where is that place?"

"I think that's enough exposition, don't you?" He sips his drink. "Which just leaves us the question of what now to do with *you*. Can't have you wandering about with all this in your head, can we?" He glances at the man in black, who is still poking ruminatively at the fireplace. "It's a real shame.

Camillo tells me you had great potential. We shall have to find another service for you to perform, I'm afraid."

There is a little tap at the door leading to the stairway, and she turns to see it open unbidden.

In steps Denton.

"Ah," says Friedler, "the very man."

CHAPTER EIGHT

SHE WAS SMALLER than Caulden had expected – petite, almost, a perfect figure in miniature, an effect exaggerated no doubt by the large, empty space of which she was the lone central feature, sat on her own mini-replica throne and dais. But maybe this was just a psychological hangover, an effect of the contrast between the enormous statue of her outside of this . . . what? Some sort of temple? Throne room? It was surprisingly spartan, given all the techno-jungle craziness outside, of which merely a trace remained in the form of a subtle patterning of the otherwise plain, level floor. He could dimly make out other decoration, far out on the peripheral walls – some Egyptian tomb or Bayeux Tapestry style comic strip? – which the weak amber lighting didn't allow him to decipher from that distance.

And then it occurred to him: there was some horrible trick at work here, a reversal of the small and the big, and it was the human sized figure they were walking toward that was the mechanical puppet, and the monumental figure above them that was the actual living original. Or then again, perhaps neither was real – or both were.

[*You are right,*] the seated figure told him, as they came to a stop some yards before her, evidently possessed of the same telepathic skills as his guide, the same bone-reverberating voice. [*We are all one. And all are We.*] Her three—well, *six* eyes observed him. [*We see that this thought displeases you.*]

The royal We.

"Well, it's not so much *displeasure* as . . . I . . ."

[*We understand.*] She nodded slowly, sending the antennae-like appurtenances sprouting from her temples bobbing and swaying. [*You are bothered by Our lack of individuality. You may speak freely. There is no possibility of offence.*]

"It's just that, Your . . ." Majesty? "I . . . it's true that our culture prizes individuality. We . . . to us, there is really no such thing as society." My god, where had he dug that up from?

The Queen nodded as if in understanding.

[*We have studied you closely. You see yourselves as driven by the competitive spirit,*] she said, [*as shaped by the natural battle for survival. But you must see that this belief is incompatible with individualism. Nature does not know individuals. Only the totality exists. Only the We.*]

Compared to his guide's, her "voice" was mellifluous, almost too comforting – a caricature of femininity – but slipping occasionally into a gravelliness, as if, guided by anxious PR specialists, she had tried to reinvent herself as the softly spoken mother of her nation, yet still occasionally slipped back into her more habitual hectoring tone.

She stood from her throne and walked towards him; in tandem, he felt a rumbling shift in the huge form above.

[*Your own body proves this.*] She was close now, reaching out – she trailed a clawed hand down his arm, picking up his own hand to examine it, her touch surprisingly warm, slightly moist. [*Separateness is an illusion.*] In illustration, she traced one claw from the tip of his middle finger down to the palm of his hand. [*The pieces cannot exist without the whole. Your separate "I", your sense of a unique self, is a fiction, a fantasy conjured from distorted thinking; in reality, We are a conglomerate, a community, no one of which is regent, and each as dispensable as the other. Look.*]

She moved toward the creature, his guide, who bowed his long head before her, and pushed him roughly to the ground. She straddled his prone form with her pincer-like legs – he did not resist – and her abdomen rose above her, poised in a quivering arc, a long pointed sting emerging from its tip – which struck deep into the creature's midriff. It offered a short involuntary gasp, spasming and jolting as the light gradually disappeared from its eyes. She then commenced to eat him, the many clawed hands busily ripping, dismembering, gouging; the teeth, too, the jaw distending to better accommodate the torn-off chunks of pale grey flesh, masticating contentedly to the accompanying crunch of bone, sinew and flesh.

Even so, it was slow work, so it was lucky that she had help, as the floor, too, began to writhe, its patterning coming alive, swamping the now quickly dismembering corpse, subsuming it into a writhing carpet of tendrils and tiny creatures. Until in mere moments there was almost nothing left.

Caulden reminded himself, unreassuringly, that this could still all have been virtual, an implant hack or some other illusion, and it was almost a torment still to retain the feeling of calm that his guide had earlier imposed upon him. And from the eye of this calm, he had suddenly realised.

They hadn't conquered Nature; it had conquered them.

Finally sated, breathless, the back of one hand wiping across her gore-stained mouth, the Queen left her helpers to consume the remnants and retreated to the throne, where she sat for a moment, her head lent back, spent.

She leant forward.

[*But Nature's greatest secret,*] she eventually continued, still panting slightly, [*is that there is no such thing as death. Would you like that? To live forever?*]

Before he could answer, a spasm contracted her face, and she doubled forward; and another, and the hideous abdomen beneath her began to throb and swell, quickly engorging to twice its size, as, at its very tip, a sphincter-like eye began to open where the sting had been, and something started to emerge. The Queen was breathing hard now, blowing and gasping through gritted teeth, her many hands grasping the throne, each other, her arms flailing out, as she grimaced and grunted.

And, with a slurp and a plop, she deposited a long narrow placenta-like sack, made of the same dark, red-and-blue-veined substance as the techno-jungle outside. Still breathless, exhausted, she reached forward one razor-tipped talon and sliced open the top of the sack, revealing as the material folded neatly back the same face that moments ago she had merrily chomped into a gory pulp. Its familiar huge eyes swivelled to meet Caulden's sickened, horrified gaze.

[*You see,*] said the Queen, her breath finally slowing, [*there is* only *society.*]

BLIND BESS TURNS her unseeing, grey-filmed eyes toward Eva.

One of Azimuth's tricks?

"Eva?" it repeats. "It's me. Abi."

She does not know that name, but for some reason there is now a sudden pressure in her head, like when before the voices come. She pushes them away, down, stands back from the cage. The bear moves closer, gripping the bars with its gnarled forepaws.

"Eva, you have to listen. We're coming for you. I haven't got long. Look for my sign. Look for the ring. Remember? You know, the . . ."

And the bear's eyes defocus, look down, and it seems for a moment confused. Eva leans closer, listening, and as the blind beast scents her, ducks as with a deafening roar one huge taloned paw lunges out through the bars of the cage, slashing at the air where microseconds before her head had been – well, Orlando's head, but still, she doesn't want to have to respawn again now: she's made good progress this game.

Talking homicidal bears, Azimuth? Really? Well, well. So it wants to play dirty, does it?

Well, she'll show it dirty.

"THE INSPECTOR has requested another audience," says Caulden.

"Audience?" scoffs Friedler. "What are you, the Pope? Did *he* call it that, or do you?"

His avatar continues to parade around Caulden's virtual office as he speaks, examining the furnishings sniffily. Occasionally, little micro-expressions of strain pass over his face, and he grunts slightly.

"So what should I do?" Caulden asks. "We should be seen to co-operate."

"Should we? Seems to me we just have to stall him until his investigative ardour gives out, he hits a dead end and gives up."

"I think it may be too late for that. He knows about *Sabotage.*"

"Which is what? A word. Apart from that, he has nothing. We have the pathologist's report – and, if needs be, the pathologist himself, who can always be persuaded to amend his findings. And we've got the girl's implant back. The most he has is some vague working theory – cloning, behavioural modification. But nothing to tie it to us." Friedler picks up a glass ornament from the table near the

window – a little translucent replica of the arcology itself –
pulls another little grimace, and replaces it. "I could always
have another go at *permanent* dissuasion?" He turns to look
at Caulden, who merely exhales in irritation. Why is he so
trigger happy?

"You know, I really wish you would have consulted with
me first, before attempting something like that."

"You would only have said no."

"Precisely."

Friedler shrugs, and continues his grunting and grimac-
ing circuit of the room.

"Are you OK?" Caulden asks. "What are you doing?"

"Just a little multitasking," he says. "But I admit, he is a
bit more resourceful than I gave him credit for. Or maybe he
has more *resources*. I still need to get to the bottom of that."
His perambulations fetch him up at the desk where Caulden
has been sitting; he looks him in the face, and Caulden looks
away. "Sure you don't want me to have another go?"

Caulden shakes his head.

"Let me handle it. There is perhaps another way. I'll think
on it."

"Well, don't think too long. Wouldn't want him to actually work out what we're up to." He sets off again for another
lap. "Speaking of which, I've another for you."

"Another what?"

"For your collection."

"Oh."

"A bit too spirited for my purposes, but I assume she'll
suit yours. What should I do with her?"

"You can make the usual arrangements with Azimuth."

"As you wish." Friedler grimaces and sighs. There is the rustle of paper and the brief sound of rushing water.

Caulden ends the call.

He stands from his desk and walks over to the table where Friedler had been examining the glass ornament, and picks it up, frowning at it.

The man has all the impulse control of a homicidal toddler.

He regrets this marriage of convenience – has done so from the start. But, loath as he is to admit it, he needs him – his human networks, his useful shady people, his lack of scruple – for he could not do all this without him. It's also been difficult keeping the whole truth from him – the Queen, the other place – he simply would not understand, might even question the veracity of it, thus lending unwelcome weight to Caulden's own lingering doubts. No, as far as Friedler is concerned, the project is simply an experiment to see whether it is possible to create more Naturals.

He looks down at the ornament, which is suddenly encrusted with a dark, crystalline growth, veined with strands of electric blues and dark vermillion reds. Reflexively, he hurls it from him, where it smashes against the wall into a thousand digital shards.

He bends and examines the debris, which reveals no electro-luminescent growth, only splinters of clear glass.

Sleep. That's what he could really do with.

Were it not that he has bad dreams.

THERE IS WAR with France. Again.

Everything she tries backfires – even adopting the actual Elizabeth's successful religious policy of the "middle way". If she attempts to placate the English Catholics, she angers the Protestants; if she gives too much ground to the Protestants, then the Catholics sow discord – or, as is currently the case, go so far as to side with the nation's enemies in an attempt to overthrow the "bastard heathen sow bitch usurper" (or something like that – she forgets how the actual French phrase translates).

Maybe Eva is losing interest, and it is this that is affecting her focus. Azimuth is pulling ahead, and if she doesn't do something soon she will have to concede.

Or maybe it's the talking bear. What was all that about, anyway? And all that stuff about a sign? A ring? Abi – a name she's sure she's never heard, but which ever since has kept wriggling around her head like an earworm, surfing on the faint chorus of inaudible voices that now provide an incessant background hubbub to all her waking (and sleeping) hours.

Strangely, just after it had happened, Augustine Phillips, one of the troupe's founders, collared young Orlando in the tiring house, inquiring, in his wonderfully fruity tones, "How fares my blind queen?" – just checking on the company's ursine investment, of course, but still it had given her a moment's pause: is he of Azimuth's party? The bear-baiting venture had been Phillips' idea (though not that of the historical Phillips, for she bets she'll find no record of him ever having done such a thing). And now she thinks of it, the whole business smells fishy, for if the bear-baiting pit across the road siphons off any more theatre-goers, what will that mean for the newly constructed Globe? And with it, her key strategy? There are other theatres, of course, but she's worked hard to establish herself in this one, and if it were to close, there'll be no nobles with whom to hobnob. That's the wonder of Elizabethan theatre, of course, the social melting pot that it provides – it really is a world in miniature: high and low, rich and poor; wordplay and classical allusions for the toffs, smutty innuendo and knock-about comedy for the groundlings. But if the Globe were to close, what then will happen to the Lord Chamberlain's Men, and her access to the court through royal command performances?

And the theatres' existence is parlous as it is: the almost constant litany of puritanical outcry, petitioning the Privy Council to close down these "sewers of public morality"; the perpetual threat of plague, which hangs over every season like a lowering cloud. Which is to say nothing of the hit to receipts from the loss of Will Kempe, her star comedian, flounced off before even a single board had been trodden (but keeping the two Wills from one another's throats had proven a thing far beyond even young Orlando's powers). Her plans are hanging by a slender thread.

Urgh. Who'd be in show business?

And in all of this, the man about whom it all revolves is surprisingly humble and withdrawn. Oh, he can play a part, alright, and she's watched him from the wings as he bombasts out his own blank verse with professional vigour and precision – the chorus in *Henry V*, Adam in *As You Like It*. Never a major part, not something to draw too much attention to himself, but somewhere from which, his lines delivered, he can mentally retreat, like a general surveying the battlefield, to some vantage from which he can take notes that he will later give his fellow actors. "Young Master *Furioso*," he'd said to her (him) as Orlando had stood there in star-struck dumbness during an early rehearsal of *A Midsummer Night's Dream*, "you offend the air too much with the sawing of your hand, like *thus*" – making a cruel pantomime of Orlando's Helena's tortured love for Demetrius. "I *pray* you, suit the word to the *action*, and the action to the *word*. Curb the tempest of your fervour, so that it begets a . . . a *gentleness* that gives it . . . smoothness. Become, as t'were, Nature's . . . looking glass . . ." And she (he) had watched as a distracted look had come over the playwright, as if making other, interior notes of his own *ex tempore* advice for some future use.

But other than that she has few social dealings with the Great Man, and he few with the others in the troupe, preferring mostly to keep to himself and his teetering tower of papers – financial and literary – making excuses of ill heath to retire early from the genial gatherings that will go on to become the raucous all-night drinking bouts of company legend. Is he Azimuth's piece? Azimuth himself? She doubts it. For if there is political use to be made of such an alien intellect within the machinations of the game, she has yet to find it.

CHAPTER NINE

THE MESSAGE RELAYED, the reply is almost instantaneous.

"If the Inspector can come early this evening, when things are quieter," Caulden's virtual assistant tells Percy, "then the Director should be able to squeeze him in."

And having decided upon this – perhaps rash – course of action, while he watches the hours tick down, from the minute he leaves the hotel, to the second the water taxi deposits him at the entrance to the Arc, all Percy can think about is Rachel. Maybe it's his recent flirtation with death by mermaid, but everything is subsequently so much clearer. In some ways, it would have been better if he *had* died – better for her, but better for him too, struck down in the line of duty, posthumous heroism assured. That way, at least, they would both be spared the consequences of her finding out who he truly is; better dead than *that*, or to have to tell her the lie that he doesn't really love her anymore, just to have a reason to break things off. But then maybe that would not be a lie after all, for what sort of love takes second place to death?

Speaking of which, things may yet work out for the best; the evening is still young.

The Arc is practically deserted, as if all its life has been rerouted elsewhere. Like a museum after closing time, and he with a private guided tour, courtesy of his virtual assistant, which has received directions from Caulden's. Doors open eerily in anticipation of his approach, arrows that only he can see superimpose themselves on the floors of empty corridors swept clear of all footfall. But it is a superfluous guide, for he still remembers the way from his previous visit.

Except that, as he steps into the elevator and it begins to *descend*, he doesn't appear to be going that way.

THERE ARE SIX GENTLEMEN at the back door of the tiring house. The Earl of Essex wants to see a play, they say. And not just any old play; a very particular one.

"Verily, m'Lords? Tis an old piece," she overhears the obsequious quaver in Cuthbert Burbage's voice – a slight tremble of fear, there? But the Globe's manager as likely terrified of the meagre takings from dredging up so unfashionable a drama out of the scripts box, and that's to say nothing of the potential controversy attached, in these fraught times. "Would you not rather a comedy, m'Lords?

Or perhap a merry pastoral? A pastoral-comical? Comical-tragical? A tragical-comical-historical-past—"

"No," the voice peremptory, gruff and low. "Richard the Second. None other. Saturday next."

Eva peeps Orlando's head down the stair. He is a fine-dressed gentleman, the speaker, but there is a steely look about him; a hand on his sword hilt, the cape thrown back over one shoulder in that rakish musketeer fashion, as if already primed for action; a look that would as soon see your head on a spike as sitting happily on your shoulders.

"Saturday next? M'Lord, 'tis I fear scant time by which to ..."

She sees the man reach into his doublet and for a moment Eva's heart skips a beat – but rather than a bodkin, he produces a purse, heavy with coin.

And Cuthbert's qualms (artistic or otherwise) are immediately resolved.

"Very well, m'Lord. It shall be done!"

When the day itself comes, the auguries are not good.

She looks up at the leaden clouds. Great. The whole afternoon to be spent getting soaked, running in and out of the tiring house like a housewife on washday, because she'll have to double up – the Queen, the Duchess of Gloucester – and that's when they have a *full* complement. With three of the company bound over for alcohol inspired breaches of the peace, she'll need to take on one or two other roles too. And then there's all the extra lines to learn. She curses to herself, muttering at the idiocy that has left them so short staffed, the unusual phrase seized upon by the Bard himself (that man has ears like a barn owl): "Verily, their staffs are *indeed* short." (Always with the smutty punning. It's almost like a disease, with him.)

She's barely had time to think about the game, the bigger strategic picture. How does anyone change the world, when so much of life must be taken up with work? Who has time for statecraft, when you have to mend the costumes, run out to buy more wigs, do the pie and ale run, give the bear its medicine, feed the mastiffs, or—shit!

This is what this is!

It's the Essex Rebellion! (Well, attempted one.) Richard II! The sad tale of the vain, unworldly monarch, deposed by the Machiavellian Henry Bolingbroke (and later to be Henry IV), and intended by the Earl of Essex as a sort of rabble-inciting parable of the weak, traitorous, declining Queen (a thing later not lost on her far-from-feeble-minded majesty: "I am Richard the Second, know ye not that?").

So Azimuth is going to try to make use of this to overthrow the Queen! What can she do to sabotage that? (Pun very much intended.) Forget her lines? Well, she'll need to get a shift on (literally) if she is even to do that.

So it is with all this running through her head, while she makes her way to the tiring house to assemble her wardrobe – there's a tricky quick change in Act I, if she remembers the exits correctly, which means she'll have to wear the marshal's costume *under* the Duchess's dress in scene ii, and which is going to make her look and walk like she's padded for battle, but what can you do? – when she notices that one of the Earl's men is still standing at the back door, lingering like a detached shadow, eyeing her curiously as she runs up and down the stairs, trying to lace her own bodice. He is not the gruff speaker, but some other, more tender looking, long-haired youth, with barely a beard.

Oh God, not another dodgy proposition.

"Can I aid you, m'Lord?" Orlando asks him.

The figure steps out of the shadow, his hand lifted to her, and in doing so the light catches it, falling on a curious ring; a small bright-red stone set in a band of gold. What is . . . Has she . . . Where has she seen that *before*?

"Eva," the figure says, "you have to listen to me."

SQUIRREL FREEZES, and even Camillo for a moment pauses his maintenance of the fireplace to look up at this new arrival. Denton would not be out of place in Friedler's menagerie: the unsettling hybrid of native brutishness and augmentation, a face and form not tweaked to any conventional standards of the admirable or the handsome.

Well, well, says that face. *Long time no see.*

Friedler looks at her as if weighing her candidacy for something she wouldn't want to apply for, and turns back to Denton.

"I have another delivery for you to make," he says. Denton merely nods.

Squirrel looks to the man in black imploringly, panic-eyed. *You can't let him take me.* But his head has turned back to the fire as he recommences prodding the red-tipped poker into the revived flames with a renewed vigour.

Camillo?

"She didn't work out then, Mr Friedler?" asks Denton.

"No, sadly. But then, I shouldn't really be surprised." He looks her up and down once more. "A squirrel is not an easy animal to tame, it turns out."

Camillo!

"Her name's not Squirrel, you bloviating imbecile."

And with these words, Camillo turns and delivers the poker tip straight into Friedler's startled right eye.

There is a communal moment of stunned silence, punctuated only by the crackling of the flames in the hearth and the quiet sizzle of heated iron on flesh, and the body slumps to the floor as Camillo withdraws the poker. And the real mayhem begins.

The nearest bodyguard is the first to react, lunging for Camillo with a blade that emerges from his very arm, who in a single fluid motion swivels the poker and pivots like a fencing master, parrying the blade's stroke neatly to one side. Squirrel sees another blur of motion to her left as the second bodyguard is thrown across the room by some invisible force, bowling Denton to the floor like a skittle. But who has done that?

The chaperdrone.

[*It'll be time for you to start running, now,*] Camillo's words in her head as he and the bodyguard circle each other in a slow dance.

To where?

[*Find Abi. Tell her she has to get to the Arc. We need to free them. Now we've shown our cards, they'll move to eradicate the—*]

He parries another lunge from the bodyguard, and counters with his own, but the man's tweaked reflexes are much more than a match, and Squirrel senses that there is only one way this will end.

Who's Abi?

[*Go! Or we're all—*]

The bodyguard feints, and with inhuman speed, ducks inside Camillo's guard, and drives the blade deep into his ribs.

Squirrel screams as Camillo staggers back, clutching his side, as his opponent steadies himself for the killing blow – but stops, a look of confusion coming over his face, and dawning horror, but whatever internal spectacle Camillo has conjured in the bodyguard's mind is quickly cauterised, as the man in black seizes the moment to drive the poker up under the man's chin and on into his brainpan, before himself falling back.

Squirrel starts toward him, but something has snagged her foot – she looks down at a hand clasped around her ankle, and turns to see Denton trying to scramble to his feet, his limbs still tangled with those of the other bodyguard, whom their collision has rendered an unconscious dead weight. But his grasp is momentary, as the chaperdrone's field again seizes and lifts him into the air and flings him crashing through the doors into the stairwell. She runs to Camillo and kneels beside him where he has slumped, still clutching at his side, and from which blood is now pouring in a worryingly steady stream.

[*You have to go,*] Camillo tells her. [*Find Abi. Save them.*]

But who's Abi? And save them from what? What's there?

[*From what's coming.*] He clasps his side and grimaces. [*Tell her to tell the Inspector: they are not who they say they are.*]

She can hear noises from the floors above, and there are groans from the place where Denton has just disappeared.

With his bloody hand Camillo reaches up and shakily removes his glasses, revealing a brow creased with pain.

[*Here.*] He hands them to her. [*Congratulations. You've graduated. Summa Cum Laude. Now fuck the fuck off.*]

She looks at the glasses, and back up at him, frowning.

[*Go! There is a back way – follow the drone.*]

He pushes her away in a gesture that costs him more of his ebbing strength.

"Now!"

"I can't leave you like this."

He smiles – or attempts to.

[*That would be a sweet, if meaningless gesture.*]

"Come with me."

He laughs, and winces in pain.

[*The only coming I'm about to do is to an end, I'm afraid.*] He falls further onto his back, and she vacillates between staying to help him and heeding his commands.

There is a gradual thickening of the air as a pulse approaches down the stairwell: the house security drones have arrived.

[*Told you to run.*]

READ ON . . .

It is endgame.

As Percy heads for a showdown with Director Caulden, the Arcology may be finally about to give up its dark secrets.

But as Eva fights to regain control of her mind from the devious Azimuth, and Squirrel struggles to escape the dismal fate destined by Mayor Friedler, other forces may be at play of which none of them are aware.

And as this one enters its final, fatal stage, is another, deeper game about to be revealed?

Tidelands is an ongoing sci-fi and fantasy serial. Set some years in the future, it is a dystopian blend of cyberpunk, first contact, Lovecraftian horror and dark humour. *Part 4: The Sleepers* collects together instalments 51–64.

BUY HERE:

www.GarethSouthwell.com/tidelands-4/

LEAVE A REVIEW

If you enjoyed this book, please take a moment to leave an honest review or a star rating on Goodreads, Amazon or whichever platform you purchased it from.

ALSO BY
GARETH SOUTHWELL
THE MERRYWHILE BOOKS

Set in the near-future, the Merrywhile books are an ongoing series of sci-fi stories – novellas, short stories and full length novels – with a loose chronology, but which can be read in any order. They involve various characters and their dealings with Merrywhile Industries, a giant tech company with ambitions to take humanity to the next level – whether it wants to go there or not.

PALE KINGS

Dean's got a bit of a problem.

Just three days into his stint minding the family shop and already there's a jagged hole in the wall where the new smart-drugs vending machine used to be, courtesy of the local psychopathic heavy. But as the clock ticks down on his father's return, hope appears in the guise of an enigmatic beauty, a girl stepped straight out of Dean's dreams, proposing a wild and improbable plan that could just change all their lives – maybe even for the better.

A prequel to MUNKi, Pale Kings is a sharp-witted and comical journey into the crazy world of contemporary fine art, the illicit potential of virtual reality gaming, and the neurotic susceptibilities of robotic guard dogs.

MUNKi

Ten years after he died, Cari's grandfather is back.

Or at least, his memories are. Stolen and repackaged by tech giant Merrywhile Industries into a corporate video to promote their latest project – digital immortality.

When no one believes her, Cari's search for proof drives her into a lawless virtual underworld of hackers-for-hire where anything is for sale – and payment isn't always in cryptocurrency.

But global megacorporations don't take well to scrutiny. As Cari looks into Merrywhile, Merrywhile also looks into her.

And as she realises there's more to the grandfather she loved and thought she knew, his secrets make her a target for shadowy players in a game with stakes much higher than data theft.

CONTENT PROVIDER

His memory is not what it was.

Whose is? Sometimes, it's true, he forgets things. But writing a whole book? Who would forget that?

But there are even reviews of it. In fact, three of them. And no one – not the bookstores, not his publisher, nor even his wife – seems in the least bit concerned. Does this mean he's going crazy?

But the next one is already overdue, and though each day the screen stares blankly back at him, he must push on. For it's not like this book is going to write itself – is it?

Content Provider is a satirical insight into the life of the jobbing writer, the enduring mysteries of married life, and what happens to our thoughts when there's no one there to think them.

MR WOLF

Merrywhile is dead. Long live Merrywhile!

With the company in crisis and her boss absconded, Dr Geraldine Andersen struggles to get Project MUNKi back on track. But while her efforts to build the world's most advanced toy robot flounder, she is approached by an old friend in need of a favour. A friend whose paralysed, locked-in son is being charged with murder – of his own father. Can Gerry help prove his innocence?

But the deeper she digs, the more puzzling things become. For all families have secrets – and this one most of all.

Mr Wolf is a near-future sci-fi whodunnit, an insight into the politics of Italian refuse collection, and a cautionary tale about the lengths to which we will go to protect the things we love.

ABOUT THE AUTHOR

GARETH SOUTHWELL is a writer, illustrator and philosopher from Wales, UK. For more on all these things, please visit his website, where (if you haven't already) you can also sign-up for news, updates and the occasional free story.

AUTHOR'S WEBSITE:
www.GarethSouthwell.com

ACKNOWLEDGEMENTS

AS USUAL, LOTS OF PEOPLE were kind enough to provide valuable feedback on this book at various stages of its composition. So, my thanks to (in no particular order): Jenny Phillips, Chindilani Filifilidh Andekalithan, Michael Raymer, Lee Aspland, Phil Burton, Tess and Jo. Thanks to Eliot Southwell (www.eliotsouthwell.com) for his wonderful redesign of the WoodPig Press logo. I must also thank the Society of Authors, who provided financial support (in the form of the Taner Baybars' Award) during the writing of this novel.